TOUGH CITY
by Yuri Lowenthal and Keith Ikeda-Barry

Bug Bot Press
1335 N. La Brea #2233
Hollywood, CA 90028
orders@bugbotpress.com; http://wwwBugBotPress.com

Unattributed quotations are by Yuri Lowenthal and Keith Ikeda-Barry

Edition ISBNs
ISBN 13: 978-0-9840740-1-3
ISBN 10: 0-9840740-1-5

Edited by Candace Platt
Cover design, layout and typesetting by Adam Levermore

Printed in the United States of America

Library of Congress Cataloging-in-Publication Data

    Lowenthal, Yuri.
      Tough city / by Yuri Lowenthal & Keith Ikeda-Barry.
      p. cm.
      LCCN 2013939401
      ISBN 978-0-9840740-1-3

      1. Crime–Fiction. 2. Noir fiction. 3. Science
    fiction. 4. Suspense fiction.   I. Ikeda-Barry, Keith.
    II. Title.

PS3612.O89T68 2013   813'.6
               QBI13-600078

by
YURI LOWENTHAL
and
KEITH IKEDA-BARRY

TOUGH CITY

FOREWORD

The story you are about to read is true. It was born of madness, friendship, a dare, a sincere love for the hardest boiled of fiction, and was written entirely in seventy-two hours. The story of how it came to be may be as exciting as the story itself, so even though it's been fifteen years since it was written, I feel a bit of backstory is in order. (You can skip this section and get straight to the good stuff, but I think reading this bit will help make the book a lot more fun. And writing it just may help me open a magical door back to the long weekend in which it was written, and immortalize it forever. So if you're still with me, indulge me for a few more minutes.)

The year is 1997. I'm living the bohemian actor lifestyle in New York City. My phone rings. On the other end is a madman known as Keith Ikeda-Barry, a close friend and partner-in-crime with whom I had frequently gotten into trouble while living in Japan only a couple of years before. (If we had both stayed, we would surely be sharing a cell right about now.) The call was all the way from Vancouver, where he lived with his lovely wife (from whom he stole half of his last name). He cut right to the chase:

"This local publishing company called Anvil Press holds a yearly 72-hour Novel Writing Contest, and it's coming up. Do you want–."

"Yes," I said. That was all I needed to hear. I was in.

In short, the rules (as I recall them) were: 1) You could have an idea, an outline,but could not actually have written anything yet. (This makes it sort of an "honor system" situation, but not really. The guys at Anvil Press have been doing this long enough to recognize that when you turn in a 500-page manuscript at the end of 72 hours, you probably didn't play by the rules); 2) You could collaborate with one other person; 3) You could write it anywhere, but had to have a neutral third party act as a witness that you were following the rules of the contest; and 4) You had to be completely mad. Okay, I think I'm misremembering that last rule; it was probably more of a helpful suggestion. The contest took place over the Labor Day weekend, beginning at 6 p.m. Friday and ending at 6 p.m. Monday. (As I was writing this, I took a moment to check for the first time in years and found that the contest is still a yearly thing. You can find more details at www.3DayNovel.com. I'm not going to, because I like the way my rules sound, and they're probably close enough.)

Keith was in Vancouver; I was in New York. We would need to write together, but knew that if I went there, there would be distractions, and if he came to me, well… it's New York, for fuck's sake. We agreed to meet somewhere in the middle, at a location neither of us had ever been to before, or ever seriously considered visiting. No distractions. We looked at a map. Almost exactly equidistant from both of our cities: Wichita, Kansas. The only thing either of us knew about Wichita was that it figured prominently in the lyrics of a song on the Soul Coughing album we were both listening to. Perfect.

We booked flights. We reserved a room at a roadside motel only a mile from the Wichita airport. We were set.

We discussed what kind of book we'd like to write together. That, too, was easy. We had traded short stories back and forth in Japan, and they were inevitably filled with hardboiled detectives, bullets, and absurdity. We always wrote with Chandler's Rule in full effect: "If you don't know what to write next, have a guy walk into the room with a gun." We briefly discussed a plan of attack for staying conscious for 72 hours to get maximum writing time. We agreed that caffeine and sugar would be our fuel. Done. Also, we decided to pack anything that we would find inspirational. I dug out some recent magazine articles I had found interesting,a micro cassette recorder, and a camera. I probably packed some other stuff, too, but after 15 years, I've gotten kind of fuzzy on the details.

And then, before I knew it, I was on a plane with nothing but a grip bag full of questionable items, headed for a roadside motel in Wichita, Kansas, where adventure awaited. By the time the plane touched down in Wichita, a couple of hours before the contest officially started, I had more or less become a character in the book we were about to write. I may have exited the plane in hero-style slow motion. That's how I remember it.

Wichita International Airport proclaimed itself to be the "Air Capital of the World."I wasn't sure if that meant that they built airplanes there, or that there was literally more oxygen in Wichita. I hopped in a cab, and gave the address of the motel. I felt dangerous, mysterious, doing that. I wasn't there for a convention, or traveling with anyone else. I was headed to a dodgy motel to hole up with another guy of questionable sanity, and we were going to fuck up some shit, literarily speaking.

When I arrived, Keith was already there. Laid out on the bed were the things he had brought. Among them were two plastic ninja swords (which, this being pre.9/11, he probably carried on the plane with him). He had also bought boxes of cookies and caffeinated soda. We took a copy of the document that needed to be signed by an impartial observer to the front desk and gave it to the hotel manager—who was confused but a little bit thrilled by the prospect of having two writers use his humble motel as a surrogate Chelsea Hotel. Or maybe he saw the strange glint in our eyes, and felt he had to mirror it to placate two men who were obviously up to no good. If he reached instinctively for a shotgun underneath the front desk, I didn't see it.

There was an all-night Denny's attached to the hotel, and then nothing else for miles around. That meant no distractions, but 24-hour access to fresh coffee. This place was made for writing contests. Also, there was a sign on the door that made it known we were not to bring in concealed firearms, but that if we displayed them, that was okay. It was clear we weren't in Kansas anymore. No, wait: we actually were in Kansas for once. I guess Kansas is a lot more hardboiled than we had been led to believe. We still had a short time before the contest began, so we grabbed a booth in Denny's, chowed down, and planned our attack.

Not exactly. First we made a big deal out of telling the people who worked at the Denny's what we were doing there. And then something happened that I wish would happen more often: they got excited about it. I now live in Los Angeles. If you went into a coffee shop here and told anyone that you were there to write a book, they wouldn't be able to show enough indifference or disdain. But to Wichita, this was a big deal. If they thought we were nuts, they sure had a funny way of showing it. Many of the characters in this book (Clovis, Big Junior) are based on the people who worked at the Denny's or at the motel; and not only did we absolutely steal lines they actually said for this book, we didn't even change their names. You would think learning that at least one of these characters had done time might have been a deterrent, but no. They were awesome and supportive, and we honor them this way.

It was almost time. We headed back to our room. And then it was 6 p.m. We swore that we would let nothing get in our way. That fear meant nothing: fear of failure or fear that what we wrote wouldn't be good, or wouldn't make sense, or wouldn't win the contest. We would do this or die trying.

We gathered all of our inspirational things on the bed and started throwing out ideas. Each of us had also made a list of things we loved: from detective stories, from our favorite movies, from whatever. Random things. We were going to try to cram as much as possible of what we loved into this book, with the hoped for side effect being that writing about what we loved most would keep us awake and alive for 72 hours.

At the end of an hour, or two, or three–I can't remember, maybe it was more–we had our outline. Each section (of which I think there were 10) was written on a separate index card that was stuck, in order, onto a mirror on the wall. We each chose one to start with, and headed off to our corners where a hungry laptop awaited (a Mac Powerbook 540c, for those of you keeping score). We had coffee and sugar in easy reach. The idea was that, as one of us finished a section, he'd pull the next card and keep going.

We wrote in silence that was sporadically broken by a cackle from one corner of the room or the other. The cackles became more and more frequent as night turned to day and back again. From time to time we needed to take a break and shake it off, or occasionally up, so that we could keep going. We attacked each other with plastic ninja swords, jumped on the bed, ran around the grounds of the motel, stopped in for inspiration (and fresh coffee) from the night shift at Denny's, ate sugar packets, shotgunned Mountain Dew, and slowly but surely went madder and madder over the course of 72 hours.

And something wonderful began to take shape. Not that we knew it at the time—although, from the increased cackling, it was clear that at least we enjoyed what we were writing. It was the kind of thing that could have been created only under these circumstances, when you slam together two people, neither of whom has time to reflect on what he's just written, but who must just keep going...keep going... keep going. Sleep deprivation and sugar and caffeine and the thrill of the contest and just being two tough guys in a motel room writing a novel make a potent creative elixir.

We kept each other awake as best we could if one of us was flagging, but ultimately we had to get some sleep. How much? Well, we had only so much time to write, so twenty minutes here, thirty there; we were afraid to sleep more. I think we took a couple of short naps, maybe a grand total of somewhere between one and two hours over the course of the 72. Once again, it's fuzzy.

Here's something I do remember: at some point deep into our journey, the phone rang. It was my girlfriend calling from New York. (This was before I had a cellphone, so she had called our room–presumably with the number I had left her for emergencies.) She wanted to know how things were going, or to ask why I hadn't called to tell her I love her, or to make sure there weren't hookers in the room and that we weren't having gay sex, or to confirm that I wasn't having too much fun without her–even though I had expressly said that I would call her when I could,but that these 72 hours would have to be as distraction-free as possible. I honestly don't remember exactly what she said, and I remember even less of what I said. I was drunk on sleep deprivation and sugar and imagination. All I know is that when I got back, she was angry. She said I had sounded like a lunatic on the phone. And I'm sure she was right about that. To be sure, I had warned her.

Had nearly three days already gone by? It felt like a minute and an eternity all at the same time. As we headed into the final few hours, we realized that we had to wrap things up. Nerves set in. We kicked it into overdrive. And finished whatever it was we had created. We didn't know. We hadn't had time to go back and reread. We hoped it would work. All we knew was that we had done this crazy thing. Keith flew back to Vancouver, and I to New York, and that motel (I like to believe) was never the same. Or maybe it was just we who were never the same.

We mailed a copy of the manuscript, as promised, to the motel and never heard back. I like to believe that Big Junior gathered Clovis and the rest around a big fire and read it to them every night until the pages disintegrated, and now his children recite it from memory to their children, and so it will continue for generations.

We didn't win the contest; otherwise Anvil Press would have published this almost fifteen years ago. Being a local, Keith did some investigating at AP and was told that our book had made it into the top 5 entries of over 300 submitted. Not bad. But it didn't get us published, so the book sat. For years. But every time I went back to it, it made me laugh. It still does. So I finally decided that I had to get this book to you, whoever you may be. Call it closure if you must. I call it finally setting free a restless spirit.

Final Note:

I will always be my greatest critic, and going back though Tough City after so many years, I was sorely tempted to change things. Many things. I've become a better writer in the last fifteen years, and some of what I just reread embarrasses me.

But it also thrills me. And still makes me laugh. And makes me wonder if I'll ever be as good as I was during those 72 hours. And makes me hate myself a little when I realize how many projects I have begun but not completed since then. What we accomplished in 72 hours shames me when I think of all the time I whine about not having enough time to write, or when the fear creeps in about the outcome not being good enough.

For that reason I didn't change anything else after rereading it this time. I was afraid I'd kill the magic.

In the interest of full disclosure:

While this is the 15th Anniversary Edition of Tough City, this is the first time it's been printed.

I have, with the help of an editor, gone over what we wrote and made sure commas were where they were supposed to be, and that there weren't too many egregious or distracting errors. I also remember that after not winning the contest, Keith and I went back and added a few things here and there, but what you are about to read (or have already read, if you skipped this part to get right to the good stuff, and then came back) is what we wrote over those fateful 72 hours. Think about it: how else could something like this have come together at all?

Thanks to Wichita, Kansas. Or at least the airport, taxi, motel, and Denny's. You are as important a character in this book as the main character (who is named after you).

ADDENDUM

While I was looking for this foreword on my computer I found an incomplete earlier attempt I had made to pour out these memories on paper. I decided to include it, unedited and unrevised, for your reading pleasure:

How to Write a Novel in 72 Hours: or,
How I Lost My Mind in Wichita.

"I love y-"
-CLICK-
The dial tone echoed in my ear like an angry hornet's buzz down a long steel tube. Who had I been talking to? I looked up. The cheap motel room was a shambles. Everything looked a little too far away, and I felt like I had blinders on. Caffeine was making my teeth hurt. The room was vibrating. When had I last slept? A clacking noise in the corner reminded me of the madman sitting naked on a makeshift stool, pounding away on a little laptop. There

was a Japanese sword slung across his back. He cackled suddenly, turned to me and said, "Dog bomb!" I suddenly remembered why I was there and fell into a wicked fit of cackling myself. It was 4 a.m. in Wichita, Kansas.

Let me back up a step.

I'm in New York, where I live. I get a call from my best friend and writing partner, Keith,[1] in Vancouver.

"Yuri,[2] There's a local publishing company here in Vancouver, Anvil Press, that sponsors a Three-Day Novel Writing Contest every year over Labor Day weekend. And I was thinking-"

"Yes," I said, because I always say yes to him. The deal was that you could write solo or have one other collaborator, and that you could write anywhere in the world, as long as you did it within the time frame. You were not allowed to include any previously written material, but starting with an outline was okay. The contest began Friday at midnight, and ended Monday at midnight. The winner's novel would be published by Anvil Press.

We, like most people, were chock full of ideas for a novel. We also, like most people, never actually got around to writing any of them. Now we were on a mission. Only, where would we do it? It would have been unfair to ask Keith to come out to where I live, and I'd heard there are man-eating bears in Vancouver, so that was out. We agreed to pick somewhere in the middle. Blindfolding myself and sticking a pin in a map of North America was fun for a while, but got us nowhere fast. We finally ditched the blindfold and found a spot that looked like it was pretty much midway between Vancouver and New York City: Wichita, Kansas. Neither of us had ever been there. Neither of us had ever entertained the idea of going there. Neither of us knew anyone who lived there, or who would even own up to having visited there. There was, as far as we could tell, nothing of interest to us in Wichita, Kansas.

It was perfect.

Arriving at the Wichita International Airport on Friday afternoon the day of the contest, I walked through the terminal, noting the signs proclaiming Wichita, "Air Capital of the World." I had no idea what that meant. And I had no time to find out. I was here to write the great American Novel. And I had only 72 hours. I hailed a cab and rode the mile to the Motel 6 where Keith should have arrived a few hours before. I checked in. The look on the face of the guy at the front desk told me that Keith had already checked in. I headed to the room.

---

[1] *No names have been changed to protect the innocent. If I've learned anything, it's that no one is innocent.*

[2] *That is, in fact, my real name, despite how silly it may*

sound.

PROLOGUE

A dustguster appeared on the horizon, obscuring more and more of the sky as it rushed toward the Marquis de Gas with a big speed. Keihan snatched his Bustre Longviews off his chest and held them up to his eyes to get a better look. A dustguster from far away looks very much like one from up close, only now, at the base of the funnel, he could see what looked like a big black bullet. At that speed it couldn't have been a car, just couldn't. And cars didn't have flames coming out the back. Unless they were about to explode. He let go of the Longviews and the horizon returned to its rightful place. He followed the dust funnel down to that black bullet. No explosions.

He went to ratchet-bolt the pumps in case of trouble. Trudging over, he figurated he had about twenty minutes before they'd slide in to suck some of his prime juice. As prime as watered-down Super-9 could be. Maybe they had one of them big Yolo Huffers and would drink up all his Super-9, and he'd be able to shut down early for the day. Or maybe they'd be needin' some LubriFix and he could slick 'em up right for eight and a quarter. In any case, he was for damn sure they'd be stopping at old Keihan's Marquis de Gas. From the direction they were coming, he was the only thing between the desert and Tough City for miles and miles.

He and Bustre checked the horizon again. Well lucky damn day. There was more than one of them. Now the cloud was jumbo-sized with the black slug in the lead and some dull-colored jalopies– Tyberts maybe–riding its tail. A whole convoy. The Longviews made them look like they were fixin' to jump right on top of him, but when he switched back to eyeballin', he figured 5 minutes at least. He slapped his head at his own good luck and made a memory to thank the Lady on Sunday when he went to the Iconoplex.

Keihan strutted over to the service tower so as to be ready and fuckin' waiting when they got there. Not to mention armored and armed in case they had any not so ha-ha funny ideas. At the door of the squat, black tower, he stopped, though, because of them vibrations what shuddered him clear up through his boots. He turned, and damned if that black slug wasn't a trauma-chromed vintage Derengetyev spinning 180 through the Marquis de Gas, missing the pump stations through some act of angelic favor or some ace precision on the part of the driver. He couldn't see through the angry, reflective windscreen, but an arm was hanging out the driver's side window as the world behind the car wheeled around to face it.

The arm was on fire. No, the gun in the hand on the arm was on fire, tracing a leadly arc up the road away from it all. There was a screaming of banshees or of tires that distracted Keihan from the world-ripping sound of the explosion that buckled his knees, saving him from the brunt of the knockwave that followed more than immediately after as the first pursuer came over the hill, a fireball.

The remaining vehicles came over the rise and spun out, shredding Tarmac and bruskweed alike as they tried to keep from overshooting the sickly-black Derengetyev. Keihan scrambled for the tower like a skitterbeetle and was inside with the door sealed behind him quicker than a ponyrabbit. He bumbled up the short flight of stairs and stood behind three-enforced plexisteel, hand on the butt of the ancient flechette rifle he hadn't used since this morning. He now had a gamecaster's view of the vehicles: the black Derengetyev, precision-parked between the pumps and the two grey Tyberts–three if you counted the one that up until very recently had not been a flaming wreck–askew on the highway, engines roaring at the bit, but held at a standstill, showdown-style.

The flames crackled, the engines roared, and Keihan's heart beat heavy in his head. The screaming again, and something red emerged from the Derengetyev's cockpit that moved with the quickness of a sandspider and disappeared almost immediately in a blur towards the roaring Tyberts.

The high noon quiet descended for a moment, and then became lousy with big gunfire and a grey Tybert split, as if cut in half with a fireman's axe. The remaining revving engine suddenly thought better of a one-on-one and opened up to run, but the spider-thing suddenly materialized out of its blur and became a woman on the car's roof. All woman she was, too, with guns that seemed to be extensions of her arms, pressed against the metal dome of the Tybert. It was so odd a scene that Keihan's first thought was that she was laying on hands. They were pressed so tightly against the dull steel roof that they only burped slightly when they spoke, their soliloquy mostly contained by the grey shell, whose growl then whimpered and died.

The woman dismounted the gutted Tybert and walked leisurely back to the Derengetyev, shaking the guns loose from her hands and tossing them inside though the open window. Her hair was buoyed by the heat from her own exertion, and it defied gravity with a singular grace. She moved easily and dangerously in the simple red gown that swirled around her when she walked. Her skin was the color of chocolate Keihan had only read about in storybooks. She was the realest thing he had ever seen. She laid her hands on her own car and turned her gaze up toward Keihan, and three layers of plexisteel might as well have been crepe paper. She was fierce and beautiful, and her eyes said she was only passing through. He soiled himself with fear and fell deeply and tragically in love. The soiling was his own damn fault for being a coward, but the love was out of his control. He could do nothing else, but go down to fill her tank.

By the time he got to her car, she had already slipped back inside, and a tear of terminal disappointment squeezed itself from his eye and mixed with the Super-9 he pumped into her tank. She proffered no payment, nor would he have accepted any. This was the great love of his life, and his heart was as full as her tank. He could not loosen the grip of his hand on the handle of the pump as he inhaled the heady mixture of her spunk: cordite, burning rubber, and the fuel pooling around his feet. The Derengetyev pulled away, smooth as a lead weight sinking to the bottom of a well. Keihan's heart overflowed, igniting with his passion the Super-9 that romanced the Marquis de Gas with a cloud of flame that burned for seven days and seven nights.

ONE

My Wake Up, Time To Die alarm clock nudged me gently out of a dream I was having by trying to saw out my spleen with its Vari-Surge attachment. In this dream I was being tormented by fields of green and flowers and a gentle breeze tickling my bare toes. Suddenly having to fight off a homicidal appliance was a welcome respite from that hellish nightmare.

The Vari-Surge arm was no match for me. I got my weight over it and snapped it in two backwards over my knee like a wrestler's elbow, tossed the pieces out the window towards the curb, and went into the bathroom to patch up the few nicks and slices the clock had managed to inflict. Inflict, ha! Caress, more like. Looking in the mirror, I decided they looked good on me. I left them.

After a freeze-or-burn shower, just the way I have it, and a few vicious hacks at my face with my fuego-razor, I slipped into the rumpled suit I had left on the floor last night. I don't press my suits and I'm not impressed by people who do. Who's gonna make me press my suit, bucko? You? You and what army?

I was all out of Breakfast For Assholes and had to settle for a quick one-two fist to the gut to make my tummy stop cryin'. "A weak man's breakfast," I snarled, but it was all the breakfast I needed. No milquetoast served here, dammit.

Before I stepped out into Tough City where I goddamn live, I took a quick look at myself in the last remaining shard of a shattered mirror by the door. My suit may be rumpled, but we make each other look fucking great. I grabbed my two girls, a Dreadbolt MiniMax and a Densha 215, checked to make sure they were full, and put them to bed, one down cozy by my ankle and the other tucked away under my arm. That reminded me of something—never you mind what, fancy pants!—and I gave myself a light spraying of Bul-O-Stop before I did that step-out. I hated wearing the stuff. Made me feel soft. Weak. I caught myself with a quick right smack to the head. Only softies thought they were weak and only weakies thought they were soft. I was neither. Time to go to work.

The sun was hanging low in the sky just to get in everybody's eyes. It was really askin' for it. Boy, if I ever ran into it one day on a quiet street or in an abandoned factory, me and it were gonna have words. Words, I tell you.

The sidewalk snapped and grumped at my ankles as I stomped along on my way to the grindstone. Heavy objects flew out of windows above and smashed to the ground all around me. It was good to be alive. It was a damn sight better than being dead. Only fools die, and they die a thousand times a day. With the number of fools I met every day you'd wonder why that number wasn't higher. What the hell was I talking about? Fools are my bread and butter. You see, I'm a detective.

I stopped at a corner barricade to buy a Kill Race form from Stickie. He's a good guy, Stickie. Calls all his customers by name and knows what they want. Good with a butterfly knife, too. "Hey, Stickie," I spat out. "Got my racing form?"

"Hey, fuckface. Shove it," he rasped, passing me my paper and my regular two packs of TorquePlus Ammoclips. I flipped him a Chinese coin and split his lip for him. What a guy. They don't make 'em like him anymore. Not since the Yamashiro v. Frankenstein verdict came down ten years ago.

"One more day 'til Loose Bruce's race, huh Stickie?" I grimaced.

"Shove it, fuckface," Stickie dry-throated.

Yeah, we both loved Loose Bruce McBone, and both hated the week-long wait in between McBone's races. He really put the "kill" into a Kill Race. Him and his army of him.

"Don't take any Chinese coins," I aced as I left. Stickie snarled.

I had just passed a sign that read, "Dangerous Curves Ahead," when I noticed a fracas on the sidewalk ahead of me, blocking my goddamn way.

A good-looking young dame–which is a fine way to start a fracas in my book–was standing beside a heavy safe, half sunk in the sidewalk, hollering blue streaks up at the sky. She had a tight teal dress that cut and jumped its way around her dangerous curves, taunting me with how much fun it must sometimes be to be a dress. Her ginger curls tweaked the bastard sunlight in such a way as to make a man forget how much he hated it. The sun, that is. A man, this man, me, don't got any hate for ginger curls.

The dame in question had those legs that only come in Extra. Heartache Long. When I'd finished looking at them– which I hadn't, so wait your goddamned turn–I noticed she had a leash in her hand. I followed its diamond-studded length down from a hand made for slapping faces to where it disappeared under the safe. Her blue streak had gone from blue to cobalt, and was rapidly approaching navy. Being a detective and all, I followed the streak up to a high window. I didn't like what I saw: cops decorating the open window like ground gristle hanging out the mouth of a meat grinder. They just smiled down at the ginger dame and dropped cop cigar ash into the gap between the window and the sidewalk. You gotta hand it to the Fuckin' Tough City Police. A live grenade, that is.

"What kind of fat bastards are you?" she streaked. "What are you going to do about my dog?"

"The most common breed of fat bastard, lady. 'Fattus Porcus,'" I wised as I drew near, getting back to the unfinished business of looking at her Extra-Heartache Longs. There was still a lot of business there.

"Shove it, fuckface," she said. Well what did you know about that. We had the same paperbastard.

I walked the rest of the way to the grindstone under a hail of cop laughter, cop spittle, cop cigar butts, and the beams from the ginger dame's hate-ray eyes. She liked me, I could tell, and I decided to ask Stickie about her.

They say that Tough City is a loveless town, a place where romance goes to die. Hell, I fall in love a hundred times a day, so maybe I just do it out of spite. But it's a fake love, an 8. hour love. My heart was a stony place with few handholds for love, and so love always ended up at the bottom of a rocky chasm, broken and beaten. It seemed my heart was only a short pitstop on the way to somewhere far from Tough City. But, dammit, I had given up waiting for the Total Blam Blam, and so 8 hours was plenty enough love for me. And when Stickie got me this gal's address, I knew chances were good that she and I were going to have a De-Cameron Wichita Special 8-Hour Romance.

DeCameron Wichita. That's me.

Hey, it's a hell of a tough city, Tough City. Don't come looking for anyone to tell you different.

I got to the grindstone just as the sun chickened out and ducked behind a cloud of mustard gas. The damn weather was cruisin' for a bruisin'. Make no mistake, my friend.

And I hadn't even needed that Bul-O-Stop. I felt the weaker man for having put it on, like I do every time I get to where I'm going and don't have to shake the lead from my ugly-till-I'm-in-it suit.

My desk sits over in the corner of my office, up on its end. I don't have a lot of room for it since I had the grindstone put in. I figured since work came and went in a wishy-washy way, sitting around the office not shooting any trouble wasn't any way for a troubleshooter to spend his time. So I got something concrete that I could always count on to be there to help me fill my day: a grindstone. Two big discs of concrete on an axle and a yoke for me grab and heave-ho. When there's no work, I heave-ho.

But there would be no ho-heaving today. I stared with a hardline frown at the problem. My yoke was broke. It lay in pieces around the office. There was a piece-of-yoke-sized hole in the window through which, I suspected, a piece of yoke had probably been thrown. Like I said, I'm a goddamn detective. The rest of it was scattered maliciously about my office, shattered beyond repair like a bone from the leg of a loser who owed a loan shark. How unfunny I should think that. It was just what I was supposed to think.

There was a hundred-dollar bill stuck to the grindstone where the yoke wasn't. I knew what I'd find written on it. A nasty note from a shark written on a bank note. Trying to be clever.

Written on the hundred-dollar bill, as far as I could make out, Was, "Necks times leg." What in the hell that meant I could figure, but didn't want to. It wasn't a biomath test. It was a standard, if misspelled, threat.

And then, in addition, was scrawled, "Get the yoke, egg-grinder?"

Now if you don't think that's funny, don't sweat it, meatmouth. That's as funny and clever as a sharkboy gets. But the meaning was clear. That's right, wisecracker, I owed money to James the Beak. And now I owed him another hundred dollars to cover his sharkboy's choice of stationery. So I was no good at picking horses. Mind your own damned back-off.

My thoughts turned back to the grindstone. I had bought my grindstone from Da Cherch just like everybody else. That way you're guaranteed quality work good enough for Da Big Man Himself. You go to some queer quarry upcity and you're getting some kind of bearing-assisted, Grinds-Royce pansy-ass stone for all you know.

And Da Cherch had the best customer service around, which ain't always saying much in Tough City, but I'll tell ya, you've never seen such toughness in motion as these monks working up a sweat, and if you have you're lying like a goddamn sack. Watching them install my grindstone in the first place, I knew I had my guarantee in sweat and blood. Those monks sure know how to suffer.

But without the yoke, there would be no heave-ho for daddy. So I rung for a little religion.

"Brudda Pesto here," came back from the other end of the blower, "How can I save you?"

"You can cut that crap to start, Brudda," I said nicely. Hey, he's a man of the cloth. And don't forget it in case I ask you again later, smartguy. I just might. "This is DeCameron Wichita over in the CozTick Building. You put a grindstone in for me a few weeks back."

"Of course, Mr. Wichita. How goes the heave-ho?" He was being polite but I knew he was nervous as hell that I was calling at all.

"Nothing that we can't fix over the phone, I'm sure," I told him. "My yoke got broke. I need a new one."

That caught him off his papal guard. "Your yoke...broke? Your yoke is broken?"

"No jokin'," I said, almost enjoying it. And I would have if it hadn't been for the sharknote-note that I held in my hand.

"But our yokes are solid plexi-oak," continued Brudda Pesto, realizing that I was serious and sounding damn impressed. "You must have been spending a huge amount of time at the grindstone. Have you ever thought of joining the Brotherhood of Tough City Monks?"

I don't have to do anything I don't want to, punky, but I had to laugh at that. I told him straight. "Don't get excited, Brudda, I didn't break it through overuse. It was broken for me by some naughty boys who think they're tough."

The Brudda on the udda end of the line understood the situation immediately. Just because he's a man of the cloth doesn't make him soft on how things play out in Tough City. He lives here too, and he loads his clips one round at a time like everybody else.

"Well, it's still under warranty, Mr. Wichita. But if it was destroyed on purpose, for example as part of a campaign to regain a loan...," he petered out like a trail of blood down a dark alley.

I hate when people don't have the guts to finish their own sentences. I decided to let him stew for a minute, make him nervous. I clammed up.

"Mr. Wichita?"

I had him on the run.

"Mr. Wichita? Hello?"

Twisting in the wind like. -click-

Damn.

This meant I was gonna haveta go down and get me some religion. Now religion gives me hives. Maybe I'd just go down and squeeze the yoke outta some monks. Either way, it was gonna be messy.

I made the mess the sharkboys had left me into a tidy mess and headed downstairs. I dropped a letter bomb into the landlord's box to remind him to get the window in my office fixed. Maybe he'd think twice before letting any more sharkboys come swimming around my HQ. Maybe, but probably not.

On the ride down to Da Cherch, some young punks were teasing the convict driver of the IncarcerBus something fierce, poking at him through the bars of his control cell. Doing your time driving a bus is punishment enough in my book, and I was in no mood for shenanigans, so I made them get out. Through the rear window. At 50 mmph. Don't get me wrong, I don't ride the IncarcerBus because I need to prove I'm tough. I just am, and that means I can handle getting on the IncarcerBus.

I can also handle getting off the IncarcerBus, too, baby-boots. Thanks for wondering; next time don't bother.

As the bus took a corner at Cathedral and Seraph, the driver genuflected and gunned the engine, while I jumped off into a crowd of people gathered there. They cushioned my fall and did some falling of their own. I didn't stick around.

Da Cherch's first barricade was a joke to me. I didn't show anyone any papers, I just passed. I eyefucked my way likewise through the second and third barricades and the young friars who manned them, if you could call what they did anything for a man to do. But at the fourth Basilican Barricade, a monk the size of an extremely huge monk barred my way. There was no getting around this guy. He filled the entire passageway.

"Show me some truth," he smoothed. He was big enough to know he could smooth when he wanted. I dug out the crumpled receipt for the grindstone and showed it to him. He was unimpressed, but more importantly, he didn't budge.

"I need a new yoke."

"Don't we all, fella. Look, sinner, for all I know you could be here to do something bad," he explained. "Now show me something that tells me who you are or I'll save your soul something painful."

Oh, Brudda. A threat. From a monk. Doing security for Da Cherch. Hey, I could be unimpressed, too, when I wanted.

"You ever seen one of these before?" I asked, flashing him a

Chinese coin. I flipped it to him and split his lip. His hands balled into fists the size of Buicks and I braced myself for a collision. At the last instant he stopped and smiled.

"Ah, Mr. DeCameron," he said sweetly, prying the Buicks open empty and honest and placing his palms together. "Brudda Pesto in sales mentioned you would be coming by."

"That's right, monky-boy," I told him. "Now where is he?"

"He's taking part in a wedding service."

"Breaking his vows one at a time, is he?"

"No, no, Brudda Pesto's not getting married. We take vows of celibacy."

No sense of humor, these god-guys. "Anyone I should know about?" I asked. Hey, I'm a detective. It's my job. And besides, cash got floated around at weddings like balloons, and if you could pick out the scams, you could snatch up some of those balloons to help lighten your load. And my load could use some lightening, in case you hadn't been paying attention, mouthbreather.

"A rather influential Government Lever's daughter, apparently," said the brudda, giving away an awful lot of information for a guy with vows. "I don't know the name, but there are more bodyguards in there than Bibles. Brudda Pesto is conducting the service in the Main Chapel. Would you like to sit down and talk while you wait?" he asked hopefully, dabbing at his split lip with the sleeve of his robe. These monks don't really go out of their way to mask their game. That's what makes them such slippery characters: they don't try to be clever. I knew a Sharkboy or two who could learn a thing or three from these monks. In any case, I didn't need any saving, thanks. My soul was just the way I liked it.

"Not a chance, bub." I smiled with my teeth, the scary ones. "I know your goddamn racket and I'll have no part of it. I'll just have a walk around till Brudda Pesto's ready to see me."

"I assure you," he started, "there is no racket that-"

"Skin it, Cherchrat. We both know that bus don't stop in my neighborhood. Now you send someone to find me when Da Brudda is free, get?" He got. He didn't like, but he got.

I walked through the barricade and out towards the side chapel. I could feel the monk's eyes on my back, sizing up my soul for salvation, and it gave me the willies.

The side chapel was open, surprisingly enough, and I goddamn went in. There was gloom, a lot of red, and dark wooded furniture like pews and stuff. There was music and hubbub coming through from another part of Da Cherch. It seemed like the hubbubbsters were having a bit more fun than one usually does in a place like this. Then I smelled money and remembered the wedding. Looking to cure my case of the willies, I followed that sweet aroma across the chapel and through another door, going deeper into the cathedral. It had to be coming from the main hall. There was a hall, some stairs, some paneling and another door. I walked the hall, climbed the stairs, scratched the paneling with my keys and knocked on the door. Nothing. I put my ear to the door. Hubbub.

I thought about who I might meet on the other side of the door: guests, security bums, some tufxedo-wrapped bulletproof jerkies, a bride or two and, hopefully, a grifter or two, too. Taking money from a grifter at a wedding was like taking candy from an unarmed baby: easy and fun but with less chance of getting your skull plugged with a steelette pacifier. A lesson for you: Don't ever treat a baby like a baby in Tough City.

I opened the door and went in, ready to charm, and bully for me. I'm good at finding grifters. Hell, I'm good at finding anyone. It's my goddamn job.

And about two minutes later, I found myself in a situation, and my life was never the same again.

TWO

The main hall was soaked with security and peppered with the kind of rich people I try to avoid but usually end up working for. The kind of people who brag about living in Tough City, and get away with it because they only ever brag about it to people who don't. And most of them don't even actually live here, just hold an address in town. Usually some burnt-out building that they've never even seen. The fact that they had actually hauled their sorry asses into Tough City for this gig only backed up da brudda's story about the wedding being put on by a hotshot G-man.

The guests, riding rumor and fear of Tough City into heartbursting nerve-panic, were choked by phalanxes of bodyguards. Each group eyeballed the others with suspicion rays locked on hardburn. The gangs of security mutts were, if anything, more nervous than the guests who nestled at the nucleus of each phalanx like a cancer. The tension was as thick as the smell of Bul-O-Stop. The whole room was just a hair-trigger away from an all-out bullet festival. I felt right at home.

There was a merry gang of goons up on the stage in front of the altar. No doubt they were surrounding the groom, but I couldn't make out which one he was. The marry-me march was just starting, so I slipped into a pew to watch the parade. As I did, a wave of gunbarrels belonging to the three or four SecuriMobs nearest me swung around and stared me down with a couple hundred black eyes. In doing so, of course, they thinned out the defenses on the other sides of their squads. This led to a quick passing of the bald spot that went around for a while till it was discovered that there really was no actual breach or real increase in the threatstats. Things calmed down a picadegree and attention turned back to the aisle that the bride's mob was just then a-stomping up.

Through the legion of pinkplated bridesforcers bristling with Snubshots, I caught a glimpse of the bride. She was cute as nails in her white, pearl-riveted bawdy armor. As they passed, I caught a glimpse of her face and thought I'd seen it before. I've got a good head for faces, so I craned my neck to see if I could get another look at her, this marching bride. The wall of bridesforcers made it tough, but suddenly there was a gap and for a secasecond I had a clear view. Not clear or long enough to get off a shot, even with a Suresnipe 333—the bridesforcers made sure of that—but clear and long enough for me to see black shortsnap curls, a thick and elegant neck and kissyfist lips: Clovis.

Clovis Vroomba was getting married.

I tried to remember her parting words to me, and I didn't have to try too hard. I had told her from the very start after we had locked blocks at O'Kenko's that she'd only get eight hours, and she had taken this as a challenge. She said that it'd be different with her, that she had a feeling about me. I had a feeling about me, too, but I don't like to repeat myself. Heck, I had wanted her to be right. But her eight hours come up just like everybody else's and she had waited 'til I was out on the angry sidewalk before opening her window to holler down at me so that all Tough City could hear. She told me how she was going to get married some day to a ten times tougher man than me and that her bridesforcers would all wear pink plated armor and carry pink Snubshots. And, furthermore, if I turned up at her wedding, invited or otherwise, those Snubshots would be trigger-trained to go off in my direction and erase me with pink fragslugs.

At the time, I had thought it was just jilted woman stuff to keep me out there, with the sidewalk snapping at my ankles and tough guys sticking their heads out of windows to see what the hell all the fuss was about. I assumed that she had been making all that wedding stuff up to make herself feel better and me feel worse.

And maybe she had, but here it all was as true as Da Cherch it was in. I figured I had better keep my distance from those bridesforcers' pink Snubshots, in any case. I didn't know if fragslugs came in pink, but judging from the cashola laid out for the rest of the wedding, I was betting dollars to doughnuts they were as pink as a bunnybomb's detonator nose.

I'd never really given too much thought to Clovis's hollering after that night. I just can't pay much memory-mind after those eight hours are up. But one part of her threat had always bugged me: that she would marry a man ten times as tough as me.

Now, I'm not saying I'm the toughest toughie in Tough City, and that has jack zero to do with modesty. You see, to claim to be the toughest in Tough City means waking up every morning to deal with tough guys trying to be tougher. I don't need the extra aggravation. But let me just say that someone ten times as tough as me would be very tough indeed. That would be right up there with Loose Bruce Mc-

Bone, whom I hold in very high regard, as you may know if you've been paying one lick of attention, and if you haven't, then pay up, sucker. Everything else Clovis had promised seemed in place. I had to get a look at this groom guy.

I took advantage of the general hubbub, slipped out of the aisle, and made like I was invited. It didn't matter. Security goons trained weapons of all sorts at me as I approached the stage, and proximity alarms went off on each person I passed. I was used to being on the wrong end of guns that were smarter than the goons that held them, but I did, however, hold my breath and find another place to point my eyes when passing the Securithugs carrying HerrTriga 150s. Now I'm not a very smart guy, but you gotta raise serious questions about the intelligence of someone who'd bring a highly unstable biomech weapon to a wedding. Of course, this is Tough City, and if that makes you nervous you can catch the next bus to Easyville, leaving every hour on the hour.

The Groom's goons rearranged a little to let some light fall on him for the cameras and perhaps to reassure the Bride that her man was still in attendance. Trying to get close enough to slap an ID on this Groomarooni, I actually began to feel a bit chuffed that Ol' Clovis had actually found someone ten times tougher than me. Eh, I'd believe it when I saw it. I started to get lost in a daydream in which I was showing everyone in the room who was toughest, and suddenly I was close enough to see. My eyes saw him, but I didn't want them to. Damn my eyes.

It was Loose Bruce McBone.

I turned away from the wedding party and moved behind a huge stone pillar. I slouched against it, trying to make my brain shut up. Damn my brain.

I was hit by two things simultaneously. One was the reality that a woman with whom I'd spent one of my best eight-hour runs was about to marry a man who was like a hero to me. Hell, he was my hero, and if you wanna dig around and find some sick meaning in that, then why don't you go ahead and dig your own grave while you're busy, jacko.

The other thing that I got hit by was the ass-end of a stunwave from some kind of percussi-blaster as it barely found me behind the pillar. The wave dissipated quickly enough but left me feeling that somehow someone naughty had relocated Da Cherch bells from the steeple to my brain bone. Against my better judgment–which has never been particularly good to start with-.I stepped out to see what the hell had happened.

Apparently the original owner of that percussi-blaster had opened it up wide before yanking its chain and donating chaos to an entire hall of people. Thanks to the pillar at my back, I was just about the only one who hadn't fallen down hard in a daze. The whole rest of the room was all a-kasplutter on their keisters.

And then suddenly there was no tomorrow. Everything was now. In Megatechnicolor and Super Stereo.

A deadly red spider sliced into the room above the stunned wedding guests, who were rolling around like pillbugs on the floor. My heart stopped. Or started. From high in the ceiling's vaults she tumbled, and then swung, stretched tight on a gossamer strand which she gripped between her toes and clamped between her teeth. And fire spurted from her hands.

Stunwaved goons came unstunned and every gun in the place came up with its own rude noise all at once. The air was suddenly thick with cordite, and brass casings showered the guests and their guards and the wedding parties and their guards and the bodyguards and their guards.

The screaming red devil continued her plummet and pendulumed deliciously, as if goosed with extra grace grease, out across the platform towards the altar. She floated through a fog of projectiles, her red dress flowing out behind her like a gushing wound in the free-fall wind.

Her arms raked back and forth as black swarm after black swarm from her firey weapons rattled into the wedding audience. And still the crowd around me sent enormous waves of hot reverse-rain up towards her.

And I stood there captivated, taken prisoner, poleaxed, faced, unable to take my eyes off her.

One of the wicked sprite's arms swung around to sweep the wedding stage as she passed above it. Under the seemingly interminable flow of destruction, the red carpeted platform rippled, reared up, and peeled back upon itself. Bodies threw themselves and were thrown hither and thither. The woman's plummet slowed, and she had almost reached the ground when she suddenly bent her knees like a goddamn trapeze artist and kicked her legs out, arching her back. For a split second she stopped, right before impact, and I caught a freeze frame of her, a contorted muscle puzzle, her drop line gripped tight between her teeth, forcing her mouth into a maniacal grin. Then she shot back up toward the ceiling, pumping every inch of stretch out of that spiderthread while pumping all thoughts of anything but her out of my mind. As she rocketed heavenwards like a goddamn angel, the angry clouds of lead swung with her like spray from a fireman's hose. The firing was so thick that brass casings danced forever in the air, juggled there by bullets fired.

The most beautiful woman in the world turned her spouts of fury away from the crowd below, and up ahead of herself, into the cavernous arches of the ceiling. The holy gloom of Da Cherch was broken by a sudden ray of outside light that winked once briefly as she passed through this new hole in heaven. The light burst down through the hole and stomped straight through the shell-and-smoke-choked air like a pillar. The pillar hit me squarely where I stood and baptized me in silver.

Glass and stone rained all around me, but I didn't care. I was in love, dammit, and it felt fine. I didn't flinch. Not because I was a tough guy–which I am–but because suddenly nothing else mattered to me but her.

Everything else fell out of my life as soon as she fell in, but then she was gone, and I got that socked-in-the-gut feeling like I'd just been woken up from the best dream ever. I'd lost her. I'd lost everything.

The pandemonium and kerfuffle didn't abate all that much even after it was abundantly clear that the assassin–if that's what she was–had flown the coop clean. Small nervous rallies of gunfire still volleyed back and forth as Securithugs tried to earn their keep. And the hand-grafted hairs on those HerrTriga 150s that were so notoriously hard to stop had to keep not-stopping till they stopped not-stopping and stopped.

The crowd was a mess of battered and broken forms. But security had done their job. Two figures scrambled forth, one from the wreckage of the floor and one from the wreckage of the stage. They stood, frantic and searching, until finally the one in white squealed, "Bruce!" Loose Bruce McBone and Clovis McBone-to-be clawed over slabs of pew and ducked through showers of plaster dust and found each other. Clovis's white bawdy armor was streaked bridesforcer pink with what was more than likely bridesforcer blood. McBone's tufxedo was a tattered mess. They locked in an embrace that drew the attention of all those in the room who were still able. Except me. I stumbled out and goddamn left that place.

It was all wrong. I knew so because it all seemed so right. So it had to be wrong. Nothing was ever that easy in Tough City and nothing but nothing about love was ever right. There was one way to settle this little roundabout. I had finally found someone, someone for me, then lost her, and now I had to find her again.

And if I was good at anything, I was good at finding people. But first I needed a drink.

THREE

I was pretty. I must say I looked pretty, or at the very least, cute. You had to say I was cute: I'd a busted yer lip otherwise. 'Course the only one there was me in the mirror, and I never argued with myself. At least not if I'd been drinking, so it only stands to reason that I wasn't arguing with myself now. I was a fuckin' looker. A hot, sexy momma. A goddamn sex machine. Time to party, big boy. I looked at myself good and hard. I looked good and got hard. Teal was a good color, but not on me. God, I missed her. I missed her as hard as anyone could miss a gal they'd met only six hours ago as she swung through God's own rafters, shooting the shit out of a celebrity wedding.

I tried to plummet like she had plummeted, but I was a falling clown. I should've left the makeup well alone. I should have left the fire-water well alone. I should have left the dame with the ginger curls and the Extra-Heartache Longs well alone, but I didn't, and none of it had helped. The angel in red was still gone and I was still me, and nothing I could do could materialize her here in my room. I looked at the face of the clock, and it stared me down for the freak that I was. I figured I'd at least better take off the dame's dress and put it back on the floor where I'd found it. Its romance was bleeding to death as all last night's promises leaked out of it, and if Ginger Curls woke up now, I'd have some explaining to do. Not that I cared anymore. It had been more than eight hours since I had first seen her yelling up at those cops, and, true to form, the fire had gone out. I had known it would play out this way, but that hadn't stopped me from using her to try to forget the beauty I had witnessed back at Da Cherch. Like I said, it hadn't worked. I tried reaching for the zipper in back and realized I was gonna need help. Then help busted my goddamned door in. Big help, ugly help, and come to think of it, no help at all.

"Hey, Reekie, this guy's wearin' a dress. The dick's in a skirt! Haw!"

The smart crack came from a dumb mouth that was stuck to a weasely face that was by all accounts ugly. A face only a mother would have the strength to put down like a dog.

"We always suspected youse was some a them dress-types," the other one joined in.

This other one had glasses, but that didn't make him any smarter. I happened to know that the glasses were specially designed to make him see double. This, in turn, allowed him to shoot twice as many people he didn't like. He didn't like both of me. Much to my embarrassment, I knew these two misfights quite well.

"Yeah, one a them girl-guys!" said Stewie.

"A real set a Joe Queerlies," was Reekie's notion.

"A screamin'-"

"Shut up, Stewie," barked Reekie

"But-"

"We all gotta wear dresses when we're dead," said Reekie. "Yeah, Wichita, when we're dead!" I could follow this scene without the dialogue, but spoke anyway. "You know what ratatouille is, Stewie?"

"No, smart guy, I don't."

"You will, Stewie, you will."

"What the hell? I'll chop-" It's hard to think up witty lines in a skirt, so I was glad when

Reekie ended the lame posturing by slapping me. He grinned with bonhomie and a mouth full of shark's teeth that, when he smiled, probably made people who used words like "bonhomie" shit themselves. Guess I'm lucky I don't always say what I think.

"Wichita, youse gotta stop sayin' everything what goes through that dick head of yours. A guy what didn't know youse might think youse was a bit wacky," sneered Reekie.

"Or a priss-puppet, you slicked down-" Stewie spat, or started to, anyway. "Stewie-chan. Don't bait these yeggs. I gotta go to the can."

I was feeling generous. "Down the hall on the left, Reekie."

"Youse kiddin? I wouldn't never step to youse's piss-pail if I had the fuckin' Bay of Crapwater in my bladder, you two-bit dicks. I just wanna take care of bizness. Gawds, I swear I'll never understand why da Beak likes you so much. Maybe it's that dress. Youse gots the money you owe tucked away somewhere in that decolletage?"

The look on my face stated all the obvious I needed to state. I was too damn good at that look. I should learn to lie.

"Stewie-chan, get their dresses off. I don't feel they's takin' me serious. It's like I'm yakkin' at my old ladies."

Stewie peeled me like a banana. I tried to stand tall and defiant in my nakedness but the high heels pinched my toes something awful. Reekie took off his glasses and blinked for a moment as the number of people in the room suddenly dropped by half.

"Now I'm a happy guy. I'm told I have a good general disposition. But you're gonna haveta try harder to make da Beak happy. That's why I'm givin' you a job."

"I've got plenty of jobs," I sneered.

"You should really learn to lie," he said and handed me a photo. "That's a photo. Of a dame. Da Beak's nephew is one of them cinematic Pixiville actress-types. He needs you ta find this twist for his goddamned flick. Ya see, she skipped before it was finished. He just wants to finish it, this goddamned movie.

You're good at finding people."

"Sometimes, but tomorrow's no good. I'm going to the race. I got big money on McBone. It's a sure thing."

Reekie laughed big-bore and I could see the teeth went back for rows. I couldn't help but marvel at the work while still despising him.

"Haw haw! D'ja hear that, Stewie-chan, 'It's a sure thing!' This dick cracks me up. The only sure thing, Eight Ball, is that we'll be back tomorrow like all your bad checks." He put his glasses back on. "Now youse guys find this broad for us, or else."

"An actress? I'm no casting couch."

"You'll find her, or we'll be back tomorrow and cast. . . you. . .in a cast, ah. . .in a movie about . . . something painful."

"I don't do P-Movies."

"Well, then this is your big break, smartikoff. Here's a little dough to get you started. Stewie-chan?"

Stewie smiled, reached into his pocket, and walked over to where I stood nakedly. He pulled his hand out, and in it was a fist. He put it in my stomach, hard, and I quadrupled over. He slugged me again in the back of the head, which was damn uncalled for, and then kicked me in the gut, which I was kinda expecting, so it only hurt twice as much. I was bent in such a way that they looked like they were walking on the ceiling as they headed for the door.

"Cherchez la dame, Wichita."

"Yeah, shit shamus," Stewie piped up, and jerked his chin at me, removing his hat so as to menace me with the fin graft on top of his head. They left with a slam. I lay there like a sack of wet sponges. Mercifully, the insulting banter part of the morning was over.

"Well who woulda thought?" said a disgusted voice from behind me. "A she-shamus. Last night you seemed to understand a little better the difference between the sexes. Now you don't even know which side of the bed you left your own clothes on."

I had an answer ready for her. "Uuugh-gu-hhhhk," I said, with none of the intended effect.

"Your clothes are that ugly suit over there that used to have this hundred-dollar bill in the pocket." She waved the hundred-dollar bill that used to be in the pocket of my ugly suit. "You oughtn'ta use your money for notepaper, scribble-baby."

She picked up that teal dress from where Stewie had thrown it and climbed into it in a way that made me kind of happy to be lying on the floor. I watched as she tucked everything, including the bill, into the dress.

"I don't know which fight you lost worse," she went on, enjoying having all the good lines to herself. "The one with those sharkboys or the one with my makeup."

"And those heels don't do you any favors, ladyboy," she added cruelly, plucking her shoes from my crushed toes. The shoes went to work, making the Longs on her into the Extra-Heartache type like they never would have done on me.

She headed for the door. The clock on the wall said our time was up already. Chalk up another Wichita 8-Hour Special. I decided to be generous and let her walk out on me.

"You're out of Bul-O-Stop," she called from the doorway. The now-empty can arced across the room and knocked a false eyelash off my eye. The pain had to get in line: I was still busy with what Stewie had left for me. "Sorry I can't stay to watch you take on breakfast," she said on her way out, "but I'll lay you a fin you go down in the third."

I didn't even wait for the door to close before I had a good laugh at all of them and their tough talk. But my insides had been kicked out, and the laugh shoved me over the border into a state of unconsciousness, a state where the border guards knew me well.

FOUR

Bella Djawanna had a spot in line at the bank because she was friends with someone who had an acquaintance who was a schoolmate of someone else who owed a favor to someone entirely removed from the equation. It also helped that she was there to get someone else's money and was not interested in withdrawing any of her own. Banks in Tough City took it personally if you wanted to make a withdrawal from your own account. Take the time Bella had once returned home to find her apartment a mess, the cash in her mattress gone, and a bank deposit slip for the amount a-resting on her mattress like a goddamn parking ticket. "Forcible deposit," the bank called it. You were better off getting your money stolen from you the honest way, at knifepoint in an alley. At least it was a fair fight.

She held a payment chit given to her by one Festus LaSiv for "services rendered in the field of performing in a motion picture." It might as well have said that the money was for taking her clothes off in front of a camera and using her years of "acting training" to keep from throwing up during hump sessions, but then that would have been the truth, which never rings quite as true as a hastily constructed lie.

Bella didn't give a good goddamn about what the chit was for, but she knew she had had a bit too much truth in the recent lately. The truth was that the porno she'd signed onto had a surprise ending that didn't much agree with her credo, and she had fucked off in the middle of the shoot, hardly stopping to throw on a shirt before she was squeezing out the bathroom window of the "studio" and over the low wall in back that separated the motel from the terminally grid-locked beltway. Moms and Pops had brought her up with a healthy respect and plenty of know-how when it came to the old mommy-and-daddy dance, but there was so much more out there than they could ever have hoped to teach her in rural Puttenhut, and Bella had found out how ugly it could get.

Bella looked at the chit and prayed that LaSiv hadn't had the time or the wherewithal to redflag it. She considered her options: If the chit was no good, she'd have to leave the City for a while. Festy had the clout to hunt her down if it was worth it to him, and the proud part of her said it was. But that was the least desirable option. She had left her home and come to Tough City for a reason, and damned if she was going to leave now. With the money, she had a chance to lay low. Without it, she was as out in the open as a piano in a pongberry patch.

She pushed the chit through a small grate where it fell into a drawer that was pulled back through a foot of plex-isteel that thankfully distorted the all-too-crisp figure behind it. In this way, it almost made him look human.

Because sound just couldn't find its way though a foot of solid plexisteel, no matter how hard it sounded, the man made the Banquarian sign for "I.D." which Bella then pressed up against the window. He pressed his nose against the inside and squinted, then shook his head and pointed at his eyes which is the Banquarian sign for, "I can't recognize your picture through a foot of plexisteel." Bella attempted what she hoped was the Banquarian sign for, "Just give me my fucking money or I'll be waiting for you in the parking lot after your shift with a bat."

The teller just shrugged, returned the chit to Bella and pushed the button that called the next person in line. Bella stood her ground, and the teller's face got sour. No fucking way was she leaving without her money. No fucking way was she getting on a bus back home. Two mountainous security guards began to move towards her. She looked dejectedly at the teller as the guards surrounded her. Her shoulders dropped and she looked as if she were about to cry, which is why it was such a surprise for everyone to see Bella suddenly holding both guards' guns in her hands. She stuck the stub-ugly barrels up to their respective eyes, which was, funnily enough, not very respectful at all, and yelled commandingly, "What loads are these packing?"

The guards must not have heard her because they said nothing at all.

"Let's see, then."

She walked up close to the teller's window, keeping one gun trained on the two frozen security guards. They must have been frozen because they moved not at all.

She placed the barrel of the other gun against the foot of plexisteel and pulled the trigger. The noise was huge, but the window held. The guards looked at each other and then back at Bella. She pulled the trigger again. The window held, but now showed slight signs of point-blank trauma. Hairline fractures radiated outward from a blackened blastpoint. The teller sat smugly inside tapping his finger on the counter.

She yanked the trigger again and again until the booming became clicking.

The guards weren't even looking at her anymore. They had become distracted by the people with masks and guns behind Bella. Bella was getting a bit miffed. "What's a girl gotta do in Tough City to get some attention?" she wondered.

A tap on her shoulder made her spin around. She stopped just short of shooting a man whose winter hat must have fallen down over his eyes. "That's funny," she thought. "It's not even cold out."

"Hey!" he said.

He was holding an impressive gun, but it was pointed up in the air. Not that it mattered, really, as Bella counted seven other people with masks standing behind him with even more impressive guns that were pointed right at her. She was confused. They didn't look like guards.

"Calm down," said Winter Hat. "I appreciate your initiative, but we don't have time for lone gunmen. Now either take up a position by the door or stand in the corner out of the way."

He signaled sharply to the rest of his armed winter vacationeers, and like a well-oiled, spring-loaded thief machine, the band split into teams and got to work. As they attacked the vault, the locks and security devices stood aside one by one as if to say, "Pardon us, we were just joking." The thieves looked great. It was like watching old vids of synchronized swimming. Bella got the feeling that it was oddly familiar, like she was having deja vu. And one of them, cold and professional, was recording it all with a camera for posterity.

Bella looked at the window she had so righteously abused with her stolen firearm. Blackened and cracked, one more shot would have caved it. The teller seemed to appreciate this and sat with arms raised up to heaven, noticeably less smug than a few rounds earlier. She raised the gun that wasn't empty and waved it vaguely in his direction. The teller fell over onto the floor. Ha. The tapping on her shoulder again, this time softer. She turned. He was still holding his gun in one hand, but in the other outstretched hand he held out to her a bulging bag. The bag had printed on it the word "Moolah," so she didn't have to ask the "What's this?" question. She took it, and he motioned for her to come along so that they all might escape capture and most definite incarceration by the Fuckin' Tough City Police. She could tell he was smiling, even under that out-of-season ski mask of his.

"You're robbing this bank, aren't you?" she asked unnecessarily.

"Money," he responded a little too quickly. "The stuff you never have enough of. Little things with some guy's picture on 'em that men slave for, commit crimes for, die for. It's single-handedly caused more trouble in the world than anything else ever invented. Simply because there's too little of it."

"DETOUR," she said. "Seen it. It sounds like you've been rehearsing that line."

"Yeah, but I didn't actually think I'd get to use it," he replied, a bit sheepishly.

"You guys are all actors, aren't you?"

"Some of us. But we're all in the game. Why? Are you a producer?"

"Let's get the hell out of here," she ventured. And they did just that.

Outside they hustled into the back of a big, black van that said, "Fuckin' Tough City Police" on the side, and underneath, the motto: "The Toughest Goddamn Thing About Tough City." Tires squealed and the van rocked, so that the group tumbled about a bit before they got their balance and the masks began to come off. Bella waited patiently to find out more about the people that she had suddenly found herself on the lam with.

"It's a prop car. Any hack can rent one, but we had it for a film we're working on. I don't want you to think we're professional criminals or anything."

"Could've fooled this country gal."

"Yeah, well, we've seen all the movies, and we've been rehearsing this for weeks now. We're just trying to finance this indie we're lensing, 'True Dreams.' That's the working title, anyway. This is Robert." He nodded towards the ruggedly handsome fellow seated opposite Bella. "He's the lead-slash-point-man. That's Deena. She's directing this opus and is in charge of weapons and munitions. Andy's the D.P. and logistics expert. Julie's our A.D. and demolitions wizard. Abel does makeup and hair, and Eden is costumes and reconnaissance. Up there driving is Doolie, who tag-teams craft services, transportation and getaways. I'm Greg. I gaff and take care of crowd control."

As much as Bella hated the film industry at the moment, she wasn't going to be mean. Well, a little. "I hate it when people use the word 'lensing.' It's pretentious as fuck. Where are we going?"

"Away from the FTCP good enough for you?"

"Yeah, wake me when we get there."

Bella sulked in the corner of the crowded van, but really she was happy. She was suddenly taking control of her life, and she couldn't have planned a better getaway. There was just one more thing.

"I feel obliged to tell you at this point that I'm a trained actress, a crack shot, and one hell of a hep kitten. It looks like you could use one of each. Talk amongst yourselves and let me know what you think when I wake up."

The crew looked at each other. One or two smiled. Bella closed her eyes and drifted off with the rocking of the van and the lullaby of fading sirens in the background.

TOUGH CITY

FIVE

If you're lucky, some days you can just hear the stuck-pig squeal of tires before they round the corner. On those days you may just hear the fatassed engine of some angry blackout car full of angry jackamobs before they burn up half a block of innocent citizens. Yeah, innocent. And sometimes, you can just see the barrels of a hundred guns, snubbied, longed-off, and pin-cushioning out of the angry blackout windows of that angry blackout car. And still yet, there are the days when you have only enough time to hear the wet raspberry burps and the crackly-spaks, just catch the jerkety-jerkings of those gun barrels tipped with hate-white blooms of flamalation, and feel the air ripple and spit with a quart-pack of HellzHail heavy loads. Some days you can see it all coming from so far away that you can conveniently be elsewhere when it all goes down. And other days it goes like this:

I had finally made it into my clothes and out of my apartment. First stop, as always, was Stickie's.

Stickie's kiosk slumped at a surly angle where a wide-mouthed avenue crossed a hardbitten street in a particularly hardbitten district of this hardbiting city.

The sidewalk threatened to break my ankles for me as I walked that hardbitten street. I was zig-zagging, dodging for cover like I always do, but my heart wasn't in it today. My heart was busy doing some newfangled step that I had never felt before. It was beating. Quickly. Like I mighta been excited over something–but I wasn't. Like I mighta been anticipating something–but I wasn't. Like I mighta been running from something–and to hell with you and I'll be the one to send you there if you think I anything but wasn't.

Ah, hell, who was I kidding? Me? I'm not that stupid. My heart was doing a wild, remote-controlled tango, led by a red-dressed succubus who must have been a million miles away by now. I would have cut out both my own lungs for her to be leading me in that wicked tango right here in person. Who needed lungs, anyway, when the mere thought of this woman made me stop breathing?

I was nursing and cursing those thoughts when I heard a familiar call.

"Hey, fuckface!"

Stickie.

I had walked right past his kiosk without stopping for my daily KillRace form and my two packs of TorquePlus Ammoclips.

I couldn't believe it. How could I have missed Stickie's kiosk? Thinking about froufy things like dancing, and your crazy heart and what the hell was happening to it, that's how, wimp! I was getting soft. I was beginning to think I'd need to gun-kiss my chest and cauterize my bleeding heart, but I couldn't even do that without fresh horses. TorquePlus. Two clips. Stickie. I turned back.

"Hey, Stickie!" I gravelgruffed to cover my shame, "Got my racing form?"

"Hey, fuckface! Shove-," stopped Stickie.

I looked at Stickie. He didn't look back. He was looking past me, over my brawny shoulder, into the hardbitten street. I was still thinking about my skippety-spaz heart. Must've been how I missed the stuck-pig squeal of tires as they rounded the corner. I didn't hear the fatassed engine of the angry blackout car full of angry jackamobs before they opened up on the block that I was standing on. I wasn't thinking of the gun barrels, snubbied, longed-off, and pin-cushioning out of the angry blackout windows of that angry blackout car. And I certainly wasn't thinking of how it was the last time I would see Stickie standing there, whole and hale and hearty, and handing me my paper and plugs. But Stickie was. Lucky for me, Stickie was.

He spat in my face.

"-it!"

I dove like a goddamned trick seal, the edge of the kiosk counter grating the skin off my shins as I leapt over and crashed to the ground behind it. I made a quick vendetta memo to come back and rip that counter's bastard edge off with a pair of CrowPliers for trying something like that. But that vendetta went to the bottom of the list as soon as I heard the wet raspberry burps and the crackly-spaks of a quart-pack of HellzHail heavy loads slam into that counter. I couldn't see the jerkety-jerkings of the gun barrels or their hate-white blooms of flamalation, but I knew they were goddamn there. I remembered that I hadn't sprayed with Bul-O-Stop today. I remembered why.

Newspaper shrapnel burst like snow into the air all around and above me. The kiosk rocked and shuddered with the rhythm of the HellzHail as quart after quart struck it in a sideways rain.

Out the open end of the kiosk I could see Stickie. If I had ever wondered what it would have taken to make a man like Stickie–or more exactly, Stickie–dance, I now had my answer. Stickie was dancing. Apparently all it takes is a few quarts of HellzHail heavy loads.

The jackamobs kept at it in whoopee pistolito style. What the hell were they doing? Were they parked? No one parks for a drive-by. Mind you–and you better mind when I tell you to-.young punks these days have no sense of etiquette. "Just let the man fall," I thought, wincing in embarrassment at Stickie's sad dancing. The wet raspberry belching continued at speed. "Punks," I thought, and looked around behind the kiosk counter for something to read while I waited.

I found a racing form and flipped to tonight's races. Loose Bruce McBone's name was suspiciously absent. A small byline under the heading for the sixth race said simply that "L.B. McBone" had "withdrawn" from the race. There was no other mention of him anywhere in the paper that I could see. That included nothing about the wedding, or any clues about who I'd seen there, damn her. Yes, I looked, jerky. I'm a goddamned detective, aren't I?

I couldn't understand why Loose Bruce McBone–in my book the toughest mug in Tough City–would survive a wedding day massacre only to drop out of this week's race. Of course, maybe I was feeling it myself. Maybe it was that bastard Love going and making a hard man soft. I had gotten to know a little about that in the recent lately. But McBone? I realized then that I'd never be going back to the Mortudome for another Kill Race. Ol' Loose Bruce had just slipped too far in my estimation for me to still consider him my hero. Love or no love, withdrawing from a race was low, and marrying Clovis Vroomba was lower still. Loose Bruce McBone dropped off the scene like a goddamn Bul-O-Stopped bullet.

Outside the kiosk, the boom-rippedy-rip ripped on. Paperbits whipped around in clouds, and the kiosk jumped and shuddered, but remained somehow intact. I started to rethink my vendetta against the counter's edge. Maybe I had been premature. Then again, maybe I was getting soft. I jabbed a quick one-two into my ribs to straighten shit out down there. My ribs reminded me that Stewie had already straightened shit out with them earlier that morning, and that I shouldn't go jabbing them any more.

I sighed a manly sigh and assessed the situation. A carful of jackamob punks, playing at being gangsters for a day, were trying to kill me. I was lying in a pile of old news with paper dust spinning around me in the bullet-rippled air. My guts hurt. I'd never see Loose Bruce race again. I was hopelessly in love with a scarlet-clad killer who had vice-gripped my heart and then taken off for parts unknown.

I decided to go to the movies.

But first I had to get out of this goddamn kiosk.

Stickie was still dancing. Christ, it was sad.

I hollered into the full-auto jihad above my head: "For ratssake, stop and let him fall!" And suddenly, like magic, they stopped. Stickie fell. The newspaper snow fell. Stickie fell faster–probably because he was weighed down by a few quarts of HellzHail heavy loads.

With a pathetic squeak from their Accel-O-Squeal tires, the surest sign of a juviejack, they made their punkassed little getaway. Wimps. Ne'er-do-wells. I stayed where I was for a while, looking out the end of the kiosk at Stickie's carcass. His quickstep was over and now he was sweating all his blood out onto the pavement. The pavement lapped it up hungrily.

"Paperbastard!"

I looked up.

"Hey, paperbastard!"

A tough guy looked over the bullet-chewed counter and poked his nose down at me.

"Taking a break to make snow angels?"

I looked at myself. The paper shrapnel had settled and covered me like an iced grey-and-black wordcake. I stood up inside the kiosk and brushed myself off. Some clung to my coat and must have made me look humorous to this tough guy.

"Gimme a KillRace form," he said. His smug grin was like a buttcrack and made me want to spank it with an aluminum baseball bat. I looked down at the dried-out corpse of Stickie beside the kiosk. No sense in thinking about that any more.

"KillRace form, assholeski!" the tough guy guttered.

I gave him the form I still held in my hand. "Loose Bruce isn't racing tonight," I said thickly.

"What the fuck was that?" he countered cleverly.

"I said three and a half," I told him.

He slapped a five on the counter that had barked my shins and then been rent asunder by quarts of HellzHail heavy loads. "Change, Butternut," snapped the tough guy. I fished in my pocket, flipped him a Chinese coin and split his lip for him. He stepped back and dipped his hand into his coat.

"Shove it, fuckface," I said.

Tough Guy regarded me at some length, then let his eyes fall to the countertop. His gaze swept over the whole kiosk, now groaning under the added weight of all the HellzHail it had taken on. Tough guy snapped a cracking "Ha!" and dropped his hand. He walked away shaking his head slowly and flipping open his racing form.

I got out from behind that counter and stepped over that body beside it, barely avoiding the puddle that was busy filling the cracks in the pavement.

I left after carving my initials into that counter's edge. There was barely any of it left, thanks to the bullets. Bullets, I realized, that had been meant for me. Bullets that would have punched through me like a heavyweight boxer through a Japanese screen if that paperbastard hadn't snapped me out of my stupid, soft thoughts. Thanks to that paperbastard and that counter, I was free to wallow in my own mind's mire for another day. A lucky bastard was I. But a vendetta is a vendetta, straight goods and no fooling, codkisser. Hey, I don't mess around.

I went to the movies. Like I said.

TOUGH CITY

SIX

I felt like I had traded my last dime for a nickel, and realized it was wooden—and a penny. I was wandering aimlessly, which was no mean feat 'cause I was a crack fucking shot. Deadeye Dick, they called me. Today I couldn't even find the target. No races, no grindstone, and how was I supposed to coop this dame who'd flown. The sidewalk wrestled with my every footstep, but I hardly noticed.

Now, to tell the truth, heartache was a regular day-player in my dope opera. I fell in love at the drop of hat—not mine, mind you. Hey, no laughin' or I'll break your fuckin' legs. I was a fixture in The Head Over Heels Bar, and like a hopeless drunk, I knew I was sick but couldn't do anything about it. It was like some kinda dark cloud hanging over me that always kept me back a grade. Some people in Tough City had to fight for love, dig for it, bow and scrape for it, pay for it. But not me, bucko. I got it eight days a goddamn week. And it was hell.

Half of me—who could still whip your ass—would say all tough guys are just like that. A man's love is a fruitfly span and a woman's love, Methuselah. But it's not for lack of trying, damn you. I've tried like hell to hold on to that slippery eel called love, but it always squirts away, and I wake up the morning after with my heart as empty as the whiskey bottle in bed beside me. So now I was confused, thrown because that crazy, wonderful, violent dame, that . . . angel, she still had a hold on me like lockjaw. And eight hours were long since up. It was just another day like any other day except this day was completely different because she was still in it. New tricks was knockin' at my old dog heart and I was havin' trouble finding the door.

I realized I was feelin' sorry for myself and immediately felt right at home with all the other suckers around me. Then I realized I was feelin' right at home for other reasons. I was standin' in front of my mother's house. Mutha Wichita. I hadn't seen her in days. I climbed the stairs like a pro and rang the bell and yelled, "Hey Ma!"

"I'm not your mother, you pervert junkie freak! Get stuffed!" from inside came a voice that was not unlike my mother's.

"Ma, it's me! C'mon, Ma! I know you can see me, Ma!" Oh Jeez.

"Alright Ma, it's me...," I dropped my tone, "Little Mister Bunnyhead."

I heard some dead man snicker from the sidewalk behind me and I was back down the stairs like a pro before he could get past. He was ugly, with pale blonde hair, blue eyes and freckles, and overalls that made him look just like the kind of guy who's about to get a vicious beating from yours truly. He must've been twelve, but his attitude made him look at least twelve and a half. I sized him up, and didn't have to raise my head too much to do so. I smiled broadly, the way I always do when I'm about to start swingin'.

He kicked my ass.

I remember the part about going back down the stairs like a pro, and then something about something extremely painful and painfully humiliating, and then lying on the couch in my mother's parlor with an entire carp shoved down my pants. Hey! Mom always knows best, you goddamned sex criminal, so quit the stinkin' snickering or I'll have to go out and get my ass kicked again.

"Ma, why do you always have to wait until I get my ass kicked before you let me in?"

"Oh, Dee, baby, you know, it's just gotten so goddamned tricky and dangerous out there that I can't fucking go opening the damn door for any rat bastard who says he's my stinkin' kid. When you get your lousy ass kicked, my maternal instincts kick in like goddamned jack rabbits and I know it's my Little Mister Bunnyhead."

"Ma, can't you just look out the window?"

"Oh, Dee."

That was usually about as long as conversations between me and my mother went. But then today wasn't usually. It was Tuesday.

I took the carp out of my pants and put it back in the bathtub where it lived. "Ma, what do you remember about . . . Love?"

"Well, Dee, I remember that when we were still living in the fucking Primus Building, that son-of-a-bitch moved into the goddamned apartment next door. He was always very polite and friendly until that day he found out from Doc Fokker that he had contracted radiation poisoning from your father's lousy glow-in-the-dark easy chair that was up against the goddamned wall we shared. He fucking tried to kill us that night."

"Okay, ma. Thanks. I gotta dangle."

"Dee, wait. I have some fucking thing for you." From a cupboard she pulled a steel-blue Gideon Hellbender, checked to see that it was loaded, and handed it to me. It was so damn heavy she had to use both hands. "I found it last week in a pair of your father's old pants when I was tidying up the attic. I know he'd want you to have it. I worry about you, dammit."

"Thanks, ma." The gun was brand new. And we didn't have an attic. And dad had never worn pants. I wondered where she had really gotten it from. But then, of course, she was my mom.

I kissed her on the cheek and checked to make sure that kid wasn't hanging around outside before I left.

I needed something to distract me so I could think straight. I got back on track to the movies. Besides, if I went to the office I'd have to drink, and if I drank I'd get soft and weepy. Alright, more soft and weepy, then, nosepoker. I was a big, fat Sucker, choking on a hambone of wimpiness. I started to think about looking for real estate in Sorry-Ass City.

What I really needed was to clock some goddamn time with that Angel: six or seven hundred years would probably do for starters. But where was she? Or had I just miraged her in the first place?

Would I get a chance to mirage her in a second place or a third place? Was she possibly an angel for real? And did that mean I would have to get religion to find her again? I had the feeling that God and I were going to have to have words. Big words. I looked up and couldn't imagine that a sporty guy like God would live in the darkly poisonous cloud that was the sky above Tough City. Wait, dammit! I was the one who was supposed to be such a goddamn ace at finding people.

I needed to clear my head. No, that could take a real long time. I just needed something to distract me for a bit. And a movie was that thing. Nothing like being able to laugh at other people having a tough time of it to help you forget about your own sad-pants existence.

The movie theater was just where I had left it. Ah, the good old Bacchangelica! Still as disreputable as ever, I was glad to see. I couldn't read the marquee, but I was sure it was probably showing the same damn film I saw last time I was here, which meant I was in for some good old down-home high-quality family smut. Can't bear the weak-ass shit that passes for entertainment these days. I'm a goddamn supporter of the arts, so I boosted a ticket from the pimple in the booth and walked inside. That pseudo-fake butter-flavored product smell hit me broadside, and I wrestled with it for a while. You know what smell I'm talkin' about, tough guy. It wrestled me all the way over to the refreshment stand and made me buy some rock corn before it let go.

The dame what was behind the counter looked blonde and bored and exactly like the kind of girl I would've fallen for on a day at the movies. But today was an exception. I already went over that, and I ain't doing donuts in conversation's parking lot for you, brainjob. I would have picked up on this floozie in a snippety-snap had I not found myself with a serious angel-ache. I was getting bitterer and harderer by the minute. And I liked it.

"What do you know about this goddamn movie?" I asked politely.

She looked back at me so much harder than I was expecting she might that I dropped my rock corn. It covered the floor and tidied the place up a bit.

"This film is from France and is in the original French with subtitles for viewers who can read. I guess that means you'll be lost."

"That's okay, sister. I just look at the pictures anyway."

"Good. This is a delightful film which follows the journey of a young musician in search of perfect pitch."

Well, that was all wrong.

"This used to be my favorite goddamn joint! What kind of porno parlor is this?"

"The 'not a porno parlor' kind, I guess, you fat bastard."

I was beginning to like this smart-guy refreshment girl. She had a face that reminded me not unlike exactly of a girl I had seen in a photo. A photo that was in my pocket. The photo that Reekie had given me. She glared. I pulled it out. That's right, you sick, sex criminal bastard: the photo. I pulled out the photo and showed it to her.

"This is you," I said, like a guy being completely obvious.

"O," she said, like a dame who only knew one vowel.

"ALRAYGHT, HEISTERS! EV'RYBODY DOWN ON THE FLAHR WITH YER HANDS BEHAYND YER HEADS!" said Sergeant O'Clanahan like a fucking cop with a hundred other fucking cops right behind him.

The photo-girl bolted into the theater. To say the Fuckin' Tough City Police didn't like me because I was a goddamn shamus was to ignore a larger issue. The FTCP didn't like me because I was a goddamn citizen of Tough City. They suspect all citizens are lawbreakers. And, well, they're right. I took off after the girl.

She dashed straight down the center aisle and dove through the screen. I had always wanted to be in pictures, and was without shame when it came to bad puns, so I dove in right after her.

The part I always forget about diving into the unknown is you never know whether the unknown is going to be hard or soft on your brain-box. I reminded myself to go ass-first from now on, if there was an on from now. I landed firmly but painfully on my shoulder and tried to roll out of it, whatever that means. The darkness got cracked with a doorful of light and then came back. I found the door, cracked the dark again and was outside in the back alley where it smelled bad.

I could hear the cops' choppers chopping the place up inside, and could see a clot of cops coming towards me from the other end of the alley. Between me and them was a car starting up. A nifty late model Equity Herald big-block. Through the rear window I could see a mess of blonde hair. Behind me was a dead end. It was my super number-one favorite goddamn situation. I pulled my wallet out, held it open in front of me, and said-.though it hurt to even pretend–"I'm a cop!" I rushed forward, keeping the car in front of me as long as possible and hoping it wasn't in reverse. I leaned in the open driver's side window and yelled at the punkaroo in the driver's seat, "Get ready to rocket, popstopper!" I stepped around so I was standing in front of the Herald's chromiated grille, facing the cops.

It is extremely common in the honored profession of private detecting that the shamus will have served a number of years as an official detective with the FTCP before retiring and establishing his own private investigation agency. As a result, while no longer an active member of the force, he may still maintain certain relationships with current members which make him privy to certain special favors and liberties.

I got my troubleshooter's license from the back of a goddamn comic book.

It didn't take an alleyful of dumb cops to recognize the Gideon Hellbender that I produced from under my coat. All the world in front of me started bonfireworking as the cops opened up with swarms of stingers. I pulled the trigger on the Hellbender. The shockwave alone knocked the cops' bullets out of the sky, and the recoil pushed me back, deep into the grille of the Equity Herald. I smelled cop fricassee and dropped the Hellbender. It cracked the asphalt where it landed.

"Peel, punk!" I hooted over my shoulder. The car surged forward impressively, with me stuck in the grillwork like a hardboiled hood ornament. On a straight slab of road a few miles later, I pried myself loose, scrambled across the crumpled hood, and dropped in the passenger window. From the scenery whipping by, it looked like we were headed for the outskirts of Tough City.

Besides my ever-lovin' self, there was the candy-girl/actress in the backseat and the usher-hack behind the wheel. There was nothing but a stinkin' load of quiet happening in the car as we negotiated our way safely past the Tough City Bulwarkers and out into the desert that surrounded the city.

Tough City was surrounded for hundreds of miles by nada. It was an insular little pocket of hardcore that didn't stand for wimpy things like suburbs. This vast unfriendly expanse surrounding it made it so that visitors to Tough City really had to want to visit if they planned on making it at all. We flew briefly through a ghost town, and the driver hung a sharp left. I checked out the window. It was awfully damn deserted out here in the desert, that was my impression.

I kept myself busy with some snickering, thinking about those cops and what the Hellbender had to say about them. That bastard the sun skulked low in the sky behind us like it knew something. One of these days, pal, one of these god-damn days.

We had gone far enough. I told the hack to pull over 'cause we had some talking to do. He seemed happy to oblige, though he didn't even look like he was listening to me. The car stopped and we all got out. The big air overhead was welcome after the excitement of the shoot-and-run, but I was hungry to get back as soon as possible. I was a city boy, after all. But I wasn't going back without that actress. I went over to her to feel things out.

"Stop touching me, you freak!"

I changed tactics.

"So, what's the damn rumpus, sweetie?"

"You wouldn't care, tough guy."

She was right. I was a tough guy and I liked it when people said so.

"Somebody asked me to drag you outta the woodwork. Any idea what I'm talkin' about, sister?"

"Yeah, but I'm not goin' with you, shamus."

I was about to show her how wrong she was when we both heard the same noise over by the car and turned. The hack driver had fallen to his knees and was furiously scribbling something on little bits of paper.

The girl yelled "Andy!" and ran over. I followed because what the hell else was there to look at out there?

Andy–which I was going to assume was the guy's name–was bleeding from a couple of bullet-size holes in his gut that neither of us had noticed during the ride out. Some of that cop fairydust musta got through back in the alley. We hadn't noticed 'cause his usher's uniform was all black. Probably an artist-type. Looked that way, seeing as how he was draw-ing little cartoon pictures on the backs of his own business cards. Apparently his muse was seeing the end of the line coming up and still had something to say. Never understood artists, not in a million. The girl was trying to stop the bleeding with her apron, but it wasn't working. I coulda told her that, and I wasn't even a damn psychic.

"Please-," he wheezed dyingly, handing the cards to me. "Get these back to the crew, and get-"

He got quieter. I got closer. I hate to miss anything.

"Jumpy as a . . ."

"What? Jumpy as a what?"

But he was dead, and that pissed me off.

"A what? Jumpy as a . . . a WHAT?"

"He's gone. Let it go," said the actress with a sad mouth.

I put my ear up to his blood-flecked lips and pressed down on his chest. Sometimes you can get a couple more words out that way. No soap. Someone was slugging me with cute little fists.

"What are you doing? You sick bastard!"

"Forget it. We've gotta get back to the City."

"Fuck all that. I'm not going anywhere with you."

Touchy actors. Cripes. She backed away from me, but with no real place to go. I reached into my pocket and grabbed my cuffs, sliding one around my left wrist, and tossed the other one at her.

It curled around her wrist, to her surprise, and then yanked her off her feet, which surprised her extra. She said "O!" again, like it was her favorite letter of all, and her cuff fastened itself snugly against mine. Symbi-O-Cuffs. Gotta love 'em.

I knocked her out as lovingly as I knew how and threw her over my shoulder. I fished around in my pockets using my fingers for bait but couldn't come up with my packet of

Release Treats for the Symbi-O-Cuffs. I scoped around for a Mart-O-Mart, but, like I said, the closest city to Tough City is Nowheresville. Who knew the world outside Tough City could be so tough? Okay, so I never said that using symbiorganic mating cuffs was trouble-free. I had to put the girl in my lap to get behind the wheel, but I got the Herald started and pointed it back in the direction of home.

"Nice ride," I thought, and I revved the engine like a badass. About thirty-five feet later we ran outta gas. Things were fixing to take their goddamn time.

TOUGH CITY

SEVEN

I was sitting in a hot dead car belonging to a cold dead guy, and the questions were piling up a hell of a lot faster than the answers. The unconscious broad in my lap twitched like she was having a nightmare. Things were tough all over.

It was quite a ways back to the outskirts of Tough City, and I didn't look forward to walking all that way with a hundred pounds of Little Miss Sleepytime over my shoulder. And yet that was just what you'da found me doing if you'da passed me by on that road in your losermobile. Like you'da had the guts not to pick me up. And like I'da let you.

The dead, useless jalopy, and the dead, useless Andy went bye-bye over the horizon as soon as I got it under them.

Two really boring minutes later I was still hiking down the dark road with dame spilling over my shoulder when a car broke free from the horizon in the distance. It was going the wrong way for me, but I decided it was soon to be going the wrong way for whoever was driving it. The car came closer. It was low and sleek, and while I prefer my rides big and muscular, I began to smile, thinking about how much I'd enjoy taking it off the driver's hands and putting it into my own. That reminded me that I wouldn't be doing much driving with the girl Symbi-O-Cuffed to my left wrist. I crossed the road to flag down the driver and break it to him rough-ly that he and his car were now my taxi. The car suddenly slipped over onto the shoulder and pointed itself right at me. I tensed like an alley cat to leap from what was looking to be a stone cold run-down, but there was nothing to leap to. The Densha 215 landed in my right hand like a trained bird, and I was just deciding "glass or gas" when the car slowed down sharply and drew up in front of my shins. It was a taxi.

I couldn't see through the slickblacked windows, so I waited. I waited long enough, as a matter of fact, to realize how much I must have looked like the cover of a dime store novel, broad over my shoulder, gun in hand, hat perched rakishly and coat whipping in the wind. I liked it. I liked it so much that I decided to let the driver make the first move.

It took a minute for the fat bastard to open his door.

"Ha, ha, haaaaaaaa!" he shouted, catching me off guard. He said the word "ha" like he'd just learned to laugh. "Where you going? Tough City, I betcha!"

"That's right, jerky," I said, getting back on familiar feet. "And you're taking us there."

"Ha! The truth!" he gut-laughed. "Ha, haaaaaaaaaaaa!"

He came around the car, laughed some more, and opened the passenger door. He laughed as I piled the girl into the backseat and laughed when I slunk in beside her. He slatched the door shut with a "Ha, ha, haaaaa!" He was a merry bastard alright.

"Merry bastard, aren't you?" I asked, hoping to gain some insight into the laugh track.

"Ha! Ha! Haaa! I am Merry Hashida! Ha, ha, ha, haaaaa!"

I didn't quite catch that.

"Ha! Haaa! I am Merry Hashida! Ha, ha!" he repeated unhelpfully.

"And I'm DeCameron Wichita," I dropped, taking goddamn control of the conversation. "Take me back to Tough City right a-fucking-way."

"Ha, ha, ha, haaaaaa! Yes! Let's go!" he bellowed. "And who is this girl?"

"What girl?" I stonefaced. It worked. He laughed his ass off at me some more.

"Ha, ha, haaaaaaa!" he said, "Ha, ha, ha! Ha!"

The merry bastard fatted his way around the car and piled his huge self into the driver's seat, knocking his head against the door frame.

"Owp! Ha, haaa!"

He looked around for the starter buttons, twiddled his thick fingers over them, and then waved his fingers in the air like a magic spell would get the thing started. He decided he remembered the sequence and punched it in. The engine went from zero to loud in a hot roar. He laughed in surprise and delight and just because he seemed to like laughing. This guy wouldn't last a minute in Tough City, I thought. Or maybe he would. He started the meter. We were going to have to talk about that, but I decided I'd rather talk about it back in Tough City than out here in Tumbleweedsville. The cab jerked forward and he spun it around, fishtailing. At least he could drive it better than he could start it.

"Not your cab?" I hypothesized out loud.

"Yes! Yes! Ha! Ha-haaaaaaa! Not my cab. A loaner! Ha, haa!" he replied. "My Tybert got blow up BOOM! Ha, ha, haaaaaaa!"

He seemed to be taking all this blowing up with remarkably good humor. I was mildly curious, but then I remembered that things blow up all the time. I looked around the interior of the loaner. Threeinforced glassteel windows, gun racks (empty), control levers jutting out everywhere, and a control panel with dangerous-looking buttons. The carpeting also looked stainproof.

The car was loaded with things that weren't standard issue for cabs, even in Tough City. I didn't like math, but I added some things up in my head.

"This isn't really a taxi at all," I told him, daring him to deny it.

"Haaaaaa! Yes! Yes!" he shrieked, not taking me up on my dare. Or maybe he was. I wasn't sure.

"Let me ask you one thing, if I may, before I color the windscreen brain-dead red with your headpaint," I requested, awfully politely I thought, sweetening my right fist with a couple pounds of Densha 215.

"Ha?" he ha-ed.

"How did you know we were out there in need of a cab?"

"Ha, ha, ha, haaaaaa! H-haaaaaa! Yes! Ha, ha, ha, haaaaaa! Yes! Yes! Ha-haaaaa!"

I waited for his laughter to dry up.

"Ha! H-haa, h-haa, haaaaaaa! Ha, ha, ha!" The folds around his neck shook and shimmied like a hula dancer's hips.

I looked out the window, moving my heater to the back of his fat neck. There was scenery out there, maybe trees or some shit. Maybe mountains.

"Ha, ha, haaaa! Ha, haaaa, h-haa!" He slapped the wheel and rocked back and forth in the front seat.

"Istenlay upyay, umpchay," I spat. "Sorry to interrupt your laugh-athon, but pretty please, with sugar on it, answer the fucking question."

"Yes! Ha! Answer fucking question!" he finally gave me. "Look at dash! Here! Ha!"

I leaned forward and looked where his thick finger was waving around the dashboard. I saw a bunch of little buttons, lights, screens, and crap that I knew nothing about.

"Oh, I see," I said. Goddamn, I'm fast with a cover line.

"Ha-haaa! Not see!" he shrieked. I thought he was pretty nutsy himself, and I was going to tell him so, but decided against it. He was merry enough without any extra encouragement from me.

"Ha, ha! Look and see! Ha, ha, ha, haaa!" he said. "I pick your car on scanner and I think, 'Why Tough City car so far out here?' Nobody come out here so I look to your car. Ha-haaa! Dope scope say your car have nothing gas. Soon you need cab I think! Ha, ha, ha, h-haa! Yes? Haa!"

His laughter was infectious but I'd had all my shots. I lowered the Densha 215 from his fat ear and snuck it back under my right arm where it kept me warm.

I still couldn't figure what he was doing with all the hardware, software, wetware, netware, and jetware in a cab, even if it was just a loaner.

The cab rocked as another car passed us going the other way really fast. I realized it was the only other car I'd seen on the road besides us, and started to feel a little luckier about having been picked up by this merry bastard.

The merry bastard turned his head almost full around to see the car that had passed us. Odd. He wasn't laughing.

"What's something really jumpy?" I had started to ask, when that kooky chauffeur suddenly threw the cab into a hard, screaming spinout of dust, burning brakes, and blurred vision.

I was thrown against the passenger side, and the sleeping beauty on my wrist came along for the flight. I crashed into the door, and she crashed into me with enough force to keep me thinking about my ribs for a week, and for her to stay in dreamland for just as long. The cab continued spinning, and the spin continued pinning the girl to me, and me to the door. Normally I'd have liked that being pinned together business, but right now I had other things on my mind. Besides the Lady in Red still running rampage in my tickerbox, I was beginning to get curious about what the goodgoddamn hell was going on with the driver and all this spinning shit.

The cab stopped spinning with an expert snap. We were pointing back the way we'd come, otherwise known as "the wrong fucking direction." I caught a glimpse through the windshield of the car that had passed, and then got an upside-down view out the rear window thanks to G-forces called into play by the big engine under this guy's hood. His fat lead foot on the pedal must have had something to do with it as well. It was pretty goddamn clear that we were going to catch up to the other car pretty goddamn fast. But I still had some questions.

"What the fuck are you doing?" was one of them. I asked it.

The voice that came back with the clear, no-crap explanation echoed around the inside of the car in the sudden void of laughter.

"My wife," he said, "is in that car with a man I do not recognize. I am chasing them in this car with the intent of running them off the road onto the right shoulder twelve metric miles ahead. There I will interrogate and kill the man and then interrogate my wife. If her answers prove unsatisfactory in any way, she too, will die."

That's all. No ha-has. This new guy made me forget what laughs sounded like. I wanted to say a couple of things. I wanted to say that I didn't understand, but I did. He had been very clear. I wanted to tell him to turn the fucking car around and heavyfoot us back to Tough City. I was set to prod my rod behind his ear and say something really hard-boiled that would make him point the taxi's tits back towards my town. But something about the situation made me think that it wasn't gonna go my way for a while yet. At least not for twelve metric miles, a car crash, two interrogations, and a death or two.

Suddenly I one hundred percent cottoned on to what the good Frank was going on. If I reached forward and flipped down the driver's side sun visor and saw what I expected to see, then I could kiss all chances of getting back to Tough City any time soon good-bye in a big way, honeypie. But chance, along with ass, made two things that I wasn't good at kissin'. I reached forward over the merry bastard's shoulder, flipped down the driver's side sun visor and saw what I had hunched. I didn't pucker up for a good-bye smooch with that chance, though. I just let it storm out while I pulled out a smoke. I ain't the sentimental type, ya little twisty-ass.

Behind the visor was a little card that said, "Bloodfeud Permit, Generation Class," held in place by the power of its own bad self.

I'd never actually seen one before so I tried to act casual. I flipped the visor up and down a couple of times like I was thinking about something else. I left it down and relaxed back into the rear seat. By crap I was smooth. I eyeballed the permit from a laid-back position. It was just a permit-sized card with permit-type words on it like, "Hashida vs. Bridge-field" and "Carrier: Merry Hashida, Generation Eight," but it was the king of all permits. And the muscle it packed made it strong enough to shut me up.

The powergrowl of the engine was the only voice in the car for a long time. Or maybe it just seemed long because I was trying to assimilate the new information I had just received. In any case, I had had enough silence after a while.

"Well, Merry Hashida, your English is better when you're in Bloodfeud mode," I pointed out to him, helpfully.

"Standard option," he replied in that sincere as a knife, completely laugh-free voice. There was apparently a lot more to a Bloodfeud Permit than I'd ever understand.

"We don't see a lot of you Bloodfeuders in Tough City," I said conversationally, looking around the backseat. "Especially not Generation Class." Whatever the fuck that was. I found some levers and started fooling with them.

"Tough Cityfolk have no respect for laws," he said flatly, not really dropping the newsbomb he perhaps thought he was. "Do you know," he went on, "what Generation Class Ten means?"

It was a polite question, and he asked it in a very plain, straightforward and non-confrontational way that was kind of hard for a Tough Citizen to know what to do with.

"Mm-pmfffff," I answered. I had found the lever that controlled the seat's forward/backward slide and managed to lock it with my face crushed into the back of the driver's seat and my knees behind my ears. What, you think that's some kind of funny, flappypants?

"Generation Class Bloodfeuds," he said as if reciting from the book of Bloodfeud Law, "are to include the ap-proved number of generations only, starting with the successful applicant's generation and following a forward-only generational time line. Book of Bloodfeud Law, Chapter twenty-one, Verse twelve. The Hashidas are licensed for a ten-generation Bloodfeud with the Bridgefields," he spat over his shoulder and then released the backseat with the override controls that were buried somewhere on his dash like treasure.

I recomposed myself. He seemed to be waiting for me to say something.

"Uh-"

"Absolutely not."

I wasn't sure what I had been about to ask, but I took his word for it.

With big fingers that belied pickpocket-like dexterity, he started flipping open hidden panels on the dash and driver's side door, and punching buttons. Through the windshield I could see the other car ahead of us. The other driver, the one with Merry Hashida's wife, was apparently not aware of what or who was coming up on his ass.

A long section of the left-side hood opened in a flippety-floppety motion that said it had been designed to look great while opening great as well. A chrome-covered tube rose out of the slot, swung on mechanical tricks, and lay down directly along the driver's scopeline. It blossomed as dangerous bits clicked into their proper places and became a weapon to be reckoned with. I started to get a bit itchy. Merry Hashida was all ready, set, go. We hoovered up the space between us and the target like spaghetti, and within a blinklet, he was just a big ass in our window, a big ass that didn't even see it coming.

"Let loose, man! Cut him in half!" I suggested, perhaps too forcefully. The time was now, dammit! My fingers were curled into the seat-back in front of me. All the anticipation he shoulda had but didn't was killing me.

The Merry Bastard ignored me and flicked a switch. A sudden siren scream made me spin around in a cold sweat. There couldn't be FTCP out here on this road, there just couldn't.

"What in the hell's ass . . . ?" I asked, not really sure I wanted an answer.

"Warning siren. Lawcode 17.3.8a." The merry bastard said, unmerrily.

Warning siren? Fuck these Bloodfeuding Laws. These guys weren't tough. The other car took the warning pretty damn seriously though. He swerved over into the left lane to block an overtake and slapped his thruster-pedal, trying to power ahead of us. Steelette shutters started to unfold over the delicate parts of his car's ass. The shit was on.

Merry Hashida unleashed a burst of gunfire from the nose cannon. It ripped into the trunk and sent a shower of shrapnel washing back over us. The pieces of shredded metal sparked off our glassteel windshield like fireworks.

I looked down at the girl slumped in the seat beside me. She was missing all the fun, and I thought maybe I should wake her for the good parts. Merry Hashida set loose another bunch of hornetheads on the other car's ass.

"Screw it," I thought, and let her sleep.

The road twisted, and Merry Hashida kept both his hands on the wheel, never once losing sight of his enemy. I glanced at the dash that was lit up like Tough City's emergency operator switchboard. One stack of light bars had "MMMkr" beside them. Metric Mile Marker. The bars of light rose up to eleven point five. Merry Hashida had only half a metric mile if he was going to run the other car off the road at the spot he'd picked.

The other car was swerving all over, trying to prevent us from coming alongside—which was probably a good idea—while trying to stay out of the sights of the nose gun which had opened up the car's back end in a wide and rude manner. I could see why they were trying to avoid taking much more heat in the hindquarters.

Suddenly the enemy car's ass loomed in front of us like a twisted metal blossom, ripened by gunfire. The driver had slammed on the brakes, trying to force us into maneuvering off the road. Merry Hashida was having none of it. He straight-armed the wheel into the mess of the enemy's rear. I braced myself against the seat back. We hit hard with a sound I'll never want to hear again.

The nose sunk into the ass of the car ahead with the vigor of a Junior Politician getting to know a Government Lever. The enemy tried to accelerate his car out of the twisted scrap-pile where the two cars had mated, but they were partners for life.

The readout on the dash read eleven point seven MMMkr. We were getting close, and now the two cars were stuck together. Hashida, eyes ablaze, punched the brakes and locked them.

The two vehicles immediately began to slow as one, and he leapt up in his seat, moving his large bulk with a grace and speed that would have been surprising if anything could surprise me anymore. The seals around the ceiling panel hissed, and he leaned against it with his shoulders as he stood up in the driver's seat. The panel popped off and disappeared behind us as he stood up through the sunroof, holding a cannon that would have made my Hellbender whimper. From the back seat I could see him only from the ass-down, but I heard big booms, and whatever he was firing made big, confident holes in his rival's car.

I looked down at the numbers on the dash. Eleven point nine. I figured it was time to brace myself. I slid my free hand to the seat-adjust lever and pulled the seat all the way forward again, this time keeping my face clear and my knees down. I lay down over the girl on the seat and sandwiched both of us down between two layers of comfortably-sprung upholstery. I hoped it was going to be enough. The last thing I saw as I tucked my head down was Merry Hashida's right leg coming down hard on the right side of the steering wheel spoke. We veered right towards the shoulder, and there was a metallic scream of protest as the lead car tried one final time to separate from us. But we'd started fishtailing, and the car in front had zero say in the case of Car vs. Crash.

We left the road and soared toward the ditch with all the grace of a gutshot duck as the ground fell away beneath us. The cars twisted in the air as if racing to be the first to come back to earth. The seat I had wedged us into popped back and we were suddenly weightless in the back seat. Out of the corner of my eye, I saw our fearless driver catapulting through the air, having launched himself through the sun-roof upon takeoff.

Our weight came back in a big hurry, and then some. And then some more. We slid, turned over, turned over again for good measure, and then tipped up on end, pausing briefly for a spot of delicious tension–if you like that sort of thing–holding back the violence for a moment of pinched stillness. Then we slammed back down into the dirt, and I was shaken loose of our snug little sandwich.

My head hurt. My back hurt. There was some awful twisting going on somewhere but I couldn't pinpoint where exactly. There was a foot in my face. Some rat bastard was stepping on my face. I tried to send a haymaker in the direction of the rat bastard but neither of my arms was making hay today. I bit down hard on his foot instead, crunching into shoe leather. I felt pain in my right foot. The rat bastard was biting my–Oh. Damn. Right about then my brain cells decided that enough was enough and that it was closing time. That was jake by me. The last one out shut off the lights.

EIGHT

The smell of smoke was making me retch. Not the best way to wake up, in my book, but I hadn't been promised a wake-up call when I'd blacked out, and so I counted myself lucky. On the other hand, the smoke was awfully thick, and things were beginning to throb, so I decided to go back to sleep, back to where the various parts of my body hadn't been able to reach me with their express deliveries of pain-wrapped hurt-parcels. They seemed to be finding my address all too easily now that I was awake. Ah, sleep. But I couldn't sleep because of the smoke. Damn.

Well, now that I was awake, I figured I might as well go over the mental list of things to do today. I found that among such items as, "Buy Bul-O-Stop," and "Crack knuckles," was the item "Don't burn up in a fire." I promised myself I wouldn't and went to the next item, "Punch landlord." Then I backed up. "Don't burn up in a fire." Had that been on my list the day before? I didn't think so, but I wasn't sure. I was finding it hard to think straight with all of this smoke making me retch. Ah-HA! "Don't burn up in a fire," or, more specifically, "Don't burn up in THIS fire. THIS fire RIGHT HERE." Now I was getting somewhere. Hopefully somewhere away from this fire.

Unfortunately, I was having trouble finding bits of my body willing to contribute to this getting away business. I found my right arm bent way up behind me. I couldn't free it, but I found I could pat myself on the back in a nice, congratulatory way. And then, suddenly, and to my great relief, I realized I was moving away from the smoke and fire without really doing anything at all. The ground was just dragging away underneath me with a vague pulling feeling on my collar. Outstanding! No more worries.

The smell of smoke started to make me retch some more. Oh hell, not this again. I rolled over, retched, and let consciousness hammer away at my bell.

Eventually I was able to determine that the smoke was coming from far enough away that I could check at least one item off my list.

I could make out a figure moving around by the flames that danced in a long trench. The figure approached me. He laughed in a big voice, handed me some liquid in a cup, and laughed some more when he told me to drink it. If it was whiskey, it was going to kill me. If it wasn't whiskey I was going to kill him. I don't know what it was, but neither of us ended up dead, and that was alright too.

"Ha, haa! Yes, my friend! What is the name of your handlicuffs? Ha, ha, haa!" my drink-handing companion asked me. "Oh, how I try to undo you from them for getting you out of burning. Ha, h-haa, haaaaa!"

What the hell was he talking about? He was being all kinds of smart, laughing at me when I'd only just woken my broken little bunnyhead up. Maybe I was going to have to kick his ass.

That sounded about right. Maybe later.

"Symbi-O-Cuffs," I answered, instead. "Each piece can't live without the other. If they're apart when you activate them, the two pieces will clear a path through most anything to reunite."

Now what in the name of cherry-flavored hellfire was going on here? Whoever gave the okay to answer this guy's questions without talking to me first was bucking for an ass kicking.

"Ha, ha, ha! Part of you is such a beautiful bastard after headknock. Ha, ha, haaa!" said Merry Hashida.

"Don't worry, he usually fucks off pretty soon," I assured him.

Who the fuck was fucking off? Fuck! I wasn't going to spend another minute of my fucking time with these fucks. Off I fucked.

Boy, I can be a belligerent fucker. But it's part of my charm, I guess. At least I didn't wake up with that damn carp in my pants.

Merry Hashida was seeing to the still-sleeping girl who was still alive and still cuffed to me. I looked around for the occupants of the other car. No sign. There was a grip bag on the ground that said "Ransom" on it.

"So," I asked tentatively, not so eager to prompt the return of Scary Hashida. "How'd the interrogations go?"

"Ha! Bloodfeud is most complicated. Yes! Ha! Maybe you is not understand, I think. Ha, ha, ha, ha, ha!"

He shook one of his fat fingers toward the billowing columns of smoke. I followed them down into the fire trench and could make out the dark shapes of two bodies burning there, side by side.

"What's so complicated about a barbeque?" I asked.

It seemed like a lot of trouble to go through to get rid of a couple of bodies when you had a Bloodfeud Permit.

"Ha! Yes my friend! Tasty barbeque! Ha, ha, haaa!" He loved me. You could just tell. "In truth and in fact, my friend," he went on in a voice more confidential, this has been a most unfortunate error. Yes. Ha."

He had my attention. Normally I don't let people take things from me so easily, but I wanted to see how in the hell he thought he was going to get away with it.

"The gentleman who was riding with my wife was in truth and in fact her own good brother and a true Hashida feudsman. He told to me a tale of a hero before he became died." Merry Hashida's face looked momentarily solemn. "He had changed his appearance to pass as one who is not Hashida, a Bridgefield." He turned and spat over his shoulder. "His was a mission to carry money for ransom to a Ransom-Release Ceremony. For saving my wife. Yes."

I didn't get it.

"I don't get it," I said. "You mean you just killed your own wife and brother-in-law?"

"Most badly case of mistake identity. Ha," he ha'ed grimly.

"So he went to a ransom drop for your kidnapped wife, rescued the dame, snaked the ransom money AND made a clean getaway, and then you killed him in a case of mistaken identity?"

"Ha! Yes, my friend! Ha! Haaaa!"

Damn, he was a merry bastard, although I didn't see it as being quite as funny as he did. Seems like all this could have all been avoided by a phone call. I decided it was in my interest not to try too hard to understand this bloodfeud stuff.

"Yes! Ha! Bloodfeud is most complicated as I told for you Outsider to understand. Yes! Ha! Ha, ha, ha, ha, ha!"

I looked at the cars, hell-bent and melded together in a pile of debris under some trees or something. I looked another look over at the bonpyre. I looked another look at the girl who was moaning back to consciousness beside me in the other Symbi-O-Cuff. I got angry and didn't quite know why. Was it because his mistake had killed two people, or was it because this fucko might have just proved himself tougher than me? Well, I couldn't let him do that.

"So what now?" I asked.

"Ha! Ha! H-haaaa! Yes, my friend! Now it is for you to go with Big Junior back to Tough City! Ha, ha, haaaa, ha! Country life too tough for you I think! Ha! H-haaaa, h-haaaaaa, h-haaaaaaaaaa!" he said.

I didn't quite capisce, but most of it sounded okay. Who was Big Junior?

Hey.

"Hey!" I clicked in like the last brass jacket in a mag-packet.

"What gives? Country life too tough for me?" I was gonna bust his tomato. Me and my army of me with one hand Symbi-O-Cuffed behind some girl's back.

The sound of rotors came out of everywhere and some kind of contraption fell out of the sky onto the road just up the embankment.

Merry Hashida ha'ed heavily at my confusion. I had crouched by the girl and was posed for some heavy shit to go down.

"Big Junior! Big Junior! He come for take you home, Wichita!" hollered Merry Hashida over the rotornoise and in between haha's. "I call while you were out of head."

The contraption shivered on the road, rotors roaring fore and aft. It looked like a blunted silver cone with a red bulb in the middle. A small window in the bulb showed that it was evidently Big Junior's cockpit, and evidently had Big Junior inside it. The man who was evidently Big Junior motioned for us to load up.

I slapped the girl awake, quite gently, I thought, all things considered. It's amazing just how differently some people can consider things. She knuckled me upside the right eye while she was coming around. But what the hell did she know. She'd napped through most of the day. Yeah, sure, I had sold her that ticket to dreamtown, thank you very much for the memo, bub. No one said otherwise, guy. Go watch the paint dry.

We got her to her feet and I was honestly surprised that she didn't start in with the same old questions I'd have expected from a gal who'd just woken to a wrecked, burning taxi with a big guy laughing his head off over his burning wife and brother-in-law, and getting into some psycho heli-mechastrosity.

I started to move towards Big Junior's gyro-gizmo. Then came a question I had been waiting for: "What the motherfucking fuck is this goddamn thing ON MY FUCKING WRIST?"

I jerked the girl off her feet again in lieu of an explanation. I don't know how she ever got to be where she was without seeing a pair of Symbi-O-Cuffs.

Merry Hashida moved to the side of the silver cone and opened a seamless hatch that had been invisible until he touched it. The girl dug her heels into the dirt of the embankment, and Merry Hashida laughed big ha's that were immediately sucked away by Big Junior's mad whirl of rotors.

"I am not going anywhere with you, you fucker, you fuck!" spat the girl.

I lifted my left arm and swung it into the cabin. She dangled like a flunkie, and her butt found the cabin floor. I looked in. Jesus Christ looked back at me. I blinked, then I blinked again for good measure and so my eyes could adjust to the darkness inside. The aforementioned floor and entire back wall of the cabin were covered by a large blue and black blanket into which the face of Jesus Christ had been woven. I had to say I wasn't expecting the Old Jeez. The walls of the otherwise unlit cabin were adorned with small votive candles in red glass holders. It was actually kinda beautiful. I had a sudden flashback to da scene at Da Cherch and my own holy angel.

Merry Hashida looked at my face and did some more of that laughing shit.

"Big Junior is take you home! Ha! Ha, ha, haaa! Yes, Big Junior?" Merry Hashida bellowed.

I looked in at Big Junior suspended in his pilot's sling up in the red glassteel bubble that was the cockpit. Big Junior nodded bigly, as I supposed he did everything. He had iron bristles where some people had hair. I wasn't sure if this was such a good idea, but there seemed little other choice. There were no cars out here other than two wrecked ones locked in a dead lover's afterleap.

"Big Junior is ex-pro wrestle! Ha! Ha! Ha! Ex-Tough City! Ha, haaa! Yes!"

I got one foot up into the cabin, trying to keep the girl on her keister so we could get this goddamn show on the road–and by that I meant off the road and into the sky. Merry Hashida put a big hand on my shoulder. It stopped me from moving. In his other hand he had the grip bag I had seen earlier. He turned it around.

On the other side in big letters I saw the word "Ransom" again. That stopped me from asking the "What's this" question. There were still other questions, but he didn't give me any time to ask them.

"DeCameron Wichita," Merry Hashida hollered. "You had no money to pay for the cab fare into Tough City, did you?"

He was back in his Bloodfeud character, and I figured he didn't need my yapping any more now than he had earlier.

"You will not need to pay Big Junior anything. That has been arranged," he went on. "The Bloodfeud Book of Law has very specific rules about ransom money. Chapter 32, Verses 1 to 29. Technically, this money was intended for, but never paid out as ransom for a kidnapping release that did not happen. The kidnapping victim was killed while under the assumption that she was not yet freed. The ransom was stolen back from a carrier who was killed by a Hashida believing that he was a kidnapper refusing to release his victim after ransom had been delivered. Do you understand, De-Cameron Wichita, what I am saying to you?"

When I heard my name I quit looking around in the cabin for something to play with and snapped my eyes up to his. What the fuck was he talking about?

"Yeah, yeah. No one owns the money, and you're gonna give it to someone who can use it, and that's me," I boldfaced. If there's money involved, always act like it's yours. Maybe someone'll give you the benefit of the doubt someday.

"Right," said Merry Hashida.

He tossed the case into the cabin, and gave me a gentle shove with the hand that was on my shoulder. I sprawled backwards on my big fat hams.

"Ha! Ha! Ha! I see you next time driving new cab in Tough City! Yes! Ha, haaaaaaaaa!" he belted as he slammed the cabin door.

"He'd never make it in Tough City," I muttered, but I wasn't sure exactly why. "Too many unwritten rules," I smirked to myself and nobody goddamn else.

"He looked tougher than you, dickety-dog," said the girl from beside me. "Why wouldn't he make it in Tough City?"

"That mutter-and-smirk was to myself, jerky-pie," I growled. "Trespassers will be violated."

Big Junior locked the seals on the door and dropped us backwards into the darkening sky without a word of warning. I couldn't even feel the acceleration, it was so smooth. The humming of the powerdrive was a lullaby accompanying the double thub-thub rhythms of the twin rotors. I didn't know anything about heli-jumping, cone-shaped, twin-rotored flying silverfish except that I was in one. But I knew a sweet ride when I saw one.

"Sweet ride, Big Junior," I told him, leaning to peer up into the red bubble cockpit.

"Thank you," he said, turning around from the controls which were all trimmed with sheepskin. The wheel, the levers, the panels, the dials; all of them were wrapped, topped, or framed in sheepskin. It made the thing look half sheep, half toaster.

"You two are going to have to move up to the nose," Big Junior told us, pointing forward towards the narrow part of the cone-shaped hull.

I looked at the area in the nose. It was so much smaller than the cabin that I couldn't really figure out what the hell Big Junior meant. Why didn't he want us back in the cabin that looked like it was decked out all comfy-like for passengers, I wondered.

"Why don't you want us in the cabin that looks like it's decked out all comfy-like for passengers?" I asked.

"The cabin is for Jesus only," he said in a calming way that had pretty much the exact opposite effect on me.

"I'm sorry," said the goofy twist on my wrist, and she started moving backwards out of the cabin and towards the nose. As she passed me she deliberately went to my right so that I was forced to do some kind of fancy little spinning move.

When I came back around to face Big Junior there was no sheepskin-gripped PisTolOvsky pointed up my nose, but by the time I'd gotten to the end of "What the hell are you talking about?" there was.

"Please," he said. "No offense."

I wasn't sure if he meant no offense to me or if he wanted no offense from me. The baa-baa heater up my schnoz sure made me feel like giving him some.

"Jesus rides with me," he proclaimed with the kind of conviction that makes you think twice before smarting off. Hell, maybe the Jeez did ride with this guy. I just wanted to get back to Tough City.

I grabbed the ransom grip and moved into the tiny nose cone area, now mostly filled with mouthy femme, and got uncomfortable. I held the grip in my claws. I wasn't sure how far we were from Tough City, but if every passing second brought me closer to it, that suited me plenty.

"It's his chopper, DeCameron," said the girl. "He decides who rides."

I snorted.

"How much ransom money is in there?" she asked, poking at the bag.

I fumed.

"When you feel like talking," she whispered in my left ear in a sweethot way I wanted to like but couldn't, "my name's Bella."

I fumed harder, hoping the ride would take a couple of hours so that I could get good and mad by the time-. Big Junior said "We're here."

I couldn't tell where here was from where I was. I looked up at Big Junior in his sling. "Where?" I poked.

"Tough City," he said, cracking the seals with a lever over his right shoulder, but not opening the hatch just yet. He was studying his monitor screens very intently.

"Where, exactly?" I needled. I hadn't felt us touch down anywhere, but that was probably because it was such a sweet ride.

I now regretted telling him that. I wished he'd have asked me where I wanted to go. I figured we were probably still a metric mile from anywhere useful.

"Can you set us down on the roof of my apartment building?" I grumpled as politely as I could muster.

"Didn't The Hashida tell you?" Big junior asked me, taking his eyes away from the screens for the first time since we'd arrived.

Nothing good ever came out of a conversation that started like that. Nothing but nothing good. I waited, crouched beside the door with that Bella girl beside me. If bad news was coming, it was going to have to come under its own power. It came.

"I don't have an airspace permit for Tough City."

I thought about that in a couple of different ways. Neither of them was good. There wasn't a good way to think about it at all that I could think of.

"I left the Pro-Wrestle circuit to get my pilot's license so that I could someday crash a plane full of dogs onto James Da Beak's head at a heavyweight title bout," said Big Junior, blushing slightly at this personal revelation. "I wanted to get him back for making me throw my own title bout when I had such a good shot at it." He turned back to the screen. "The Beak never took me seriously until I actually passed the test and got my pilot's license about a year later. Then he used his pull downtown to get me permanently denied an airspace permit." Big Junior grinned at us.

That Bella girl grinned back, sympathetic as hell. I didn't.

"Why dogs?" asked that Bella girl. That was a good question. I had just thought it was some fucked up tough guy shit. I didn't think there might actually be a reason.

"The Beak loves dogs even more than he loves naked boys. I thought it would hurt him more if he knew that when he went, dogs would be the agent of his destruction."

Okay, so there was a reason. Big fucking deal.

"So where are we?" I asked again, getting tired of the question on my lips. It made me feel like a chump. "A metric mile away from any useful part of Tough City, I bet," I sneered.

Big Junior opened the door. I got up, dragging that Bella girl to her feet, and moved us to the exit. I expected to see Tough City in the nightsky distance somewhere. All I saw when I looked out the door was nightsky distance and a glow from below us. Way below us.

"We're as close as I can get without setting off perimeter alarms," said Big Junior.

I didn't get it. Okay, I got it, but didn't want to. That Bella girl got it for the both of us and threw up in the corner. I looked down at the glow. I had been right. We were a metric mile away from anything useful in Tough City. Like, for instance, the ground. High and dry, that's what we were.

The roof of every building in Tough City looked up at us with blank, flat faces, winking nightlights, and security beacons. I was depressed.

"Hey Big Junior," I asked, staring out at the blackness of the night sky above. "What's something that's real jumpy?"

"Gut fulla pinsnakes," he said.

"As jumpy as a gut full of pinsnakes," I tried. Nope. I was still depressed. I looked down into the city again, and as I did I caught sight of something long and black moving down one of the streets, way down below. It was two blocks long, and so I knew immediately what it was. There was only one car in Tough City that was two blocks long, and it belonged to James the Beak, my current, if indirect, employer. And, as my creditor, he was also the beneficiary, if indirectly, of anything I may earn off this job. It was a vicious funnel. It seemed that everything I had and could ever get would always go into paying for things like James the Beak's two-block-long Edison Landmass. Suddenly I had an idea. No, I just goddamn made some shit up!

"Get us over top of that fucking car! The Landmass," I told Big

Junior. He looked at his screens. "You don't have to get any lower, just directly over it."

I braced myself against the doorframe and felt the wind ruffle my hair as Big Junior banked. That Bella girl gasped, and we slid under smooth rotorpower until we were over the Edison Landmass.

"You want to get your revenge on James the Beak?" I pointed at Big Junior for dramatic effect. "Gimme a phone line."

He tossed me a phone and I punched up a number I knew all too well. It was left on my machine at least three times every week by a certain thinks-he's-clever sharkboy. I handed the phone back to Big Junior. He and that Bella girl were wondering what was up. That was soon to be the wrong direction entirely.

"Tell whoever answers who you are, where you are, and what you're about to do, Big Junior," I barked.

"What AM I about to do?" he blurted.

"You're going to drop a bomb on the Landmass," I told him. "A dog bomb."

"A what?" shrieked that Bella girl.

"Do it fucking now!" I screamed. "What kind of dogs does The Beak like best?"

"Dalmations," said Big Junior, starting to smile.

"Tell them there will be a live dalmation detonation over the main deck in thirty seconds!" I was crazed. I was hyped. I was all jacked up.

Big Junior put the phone to his ear. "This is Big Junior," he said. Then he said the rest. Then he hung up.

"What did they say?" I asked. "They said thanks for the warning and that they had a plan," he replied.

"Did they sound panicky?"

"Not really, but I'll bet they're hustling buff-boys out of the hot-tub on deck right about now." We peered out the open door of the chopper. "It's a shame," said that Bella girl, "that we don't really have anything to drop on them."

"We do," I said. And I dropped the grip bag out the door. "Wichita! No!" screamed that Bella girl. "What the fuck did you do that for?"

"I'm sorry," I pouted. "Did wittle Bewa want to keep the money? Oopsy-doodle. I'll go get it." I pulled that Bella girl to me and stepped out the door.

Who's a tough guy?

Sometimes things work out just as you plan them. Sometimes, when you jump out of a helicopter high above a city and pretend to be a bomb, things go your way just enough for you to get away with it.

Because, sometimes, if you expect the intended target of the bomb to take pity on the supposed animal cargo of that bomb, that intended target will send up a Humane Bomb Squad to bring down that bomb safely and save those supposed animals.

Of course sometimes the Bomb Squad that flies up to save you will be so upset that there aren't any real animals–I don't know, say, dalmations–in that bomb, that they beat you senseless. I know that sounds bad, but not as bad as being the captain of that Humane Bomb Squad and having to report to the guy who ordered the rescue–and who now wants to see some rescued dalmations pretty fucking quick–that there really weren't any dogs at all.

If you were, say, the captain of that humane bomb squad, don't you think it would be better to just dump the non-dog, non-bomb people you just rescued by accident over the side of whatever you were on, say, an Edison Landmass, and just phone out for some damn dogs and plastique, and just make the bomb yourself? Of course it would.

Incidentally, sometimes a tough guy who throws a grip bag full of money out of a helicopter to show how tough he is, and then jumps out after it, can catch up with that money, land safely and really impress the dame that is Symbi-O-Cuffed to his wrist.

Of course sometimes he gets the shit kicked out of him by an angry bomb squad in the process. But if he still impresses the dame, doesn't that work out to some kind of draw?

That Bella girl was quite the trooper. I had to hand it to her. I handed it to her and she handed it right back. I was in a bad way from the beating handed down by the so-called Humane Bomb Squad.

They were none too pleased with me, and instead of expressing their feelings in a scathing letter to the editor, they had chosen a much more direct approach.

Crawling out of the dumpster with Bella still attached, I declared that theirs would be the last beating I would take that day, and decided to go home and sleep everything off. There was still a lot of unfinished business, though. Like why I hadn't just turned over that Bella girl to The Beak's men when I'd had the chance.

If I'd turned her and the grip full of cash over right then, everything would have been over, and I'd be jake with The Beak. But when I'd realized that the goons on the Landmass had no clue that we were two of The Beak's Most Wanted, somehow giving everything to them as a free fucking gift just didn't seem like a good idea. I wanted just a couple of hours to sleep on all of this back at my own digs.

The digs, however, had been good and wrecked by the time we got there. I didn't care, at this point, who had done it or why. I was losing patience. And consciousness, come to think of it. In my last waking moments, I told that Bella girl the way to the grindstone. There were Release Treats there, as well as a couch. I trusted that Bella girl to get us there. I'd find out when I woke up if that had been wise.

TOUGH CITY

NINE

My head hurt. I always liked that, waking up with my head hurting. That way I knew at least that I was still among the living, my simple logic being that I just couldn't imagine that they'd have you wake up dead AND with your head hurting. That would piss me off.

So I knew I was alive, but I still had to swim to the surface. Alright, dammit, if you insist. I started to feel the rest of my body then, piece by excruciating piece. It was as if somebody had flown me out over Tough City and dropped me out of a plane.

Oh. Oh, yeah.

That brain bulletin pretty much brought me the rest of the way out of it, and I snapped my eyes open. This was, of course, too much light, and we all know that'll make the baby go blind, so I had to blink rapid-fire for a while until I got some kinda picture that didn't look like it was strobe-lit. I felt like a goddamn cave frog. On the other hand, what I felt under my back made me happy even before I could see it. It felt like my couch. The couch in my office. My office. That's right, bucko, not your office. Mine.

I opened my eyes steady and took the best look around I could without moving my neck. My desk was down on all fours again, and a vaguely familiar face was behind it.

"Morning, Icarus. Remember me?" came a voice from the face.

I wanted to, I really did.

"You saved me from the cops, cuffed me, cold-cocked me, crashed me, took me on a wacky little joyride up in the sky, and then paratrooped me against my will?" she added.

I wished I could say she was the first.

"Bella? Bella Djawanna?"

Boy did I wanna. But not just then.

Oh, right. The actress-type.

My mouth went to say: "Sorry, it's just that I'm not used to seeing anyone but me behind that desk. You threw me."

But what came out was more like: "Gah."

She got up and fetched a tumbler of water. I prayed she had washed the tumbler before she had put water in it. She dribbled some down my throat. Ah, much better. Water is good.

"Whiskey is better," ended up being my first actual words of the day, but she didn't produce any, so I just worked on sitting upright and maintaining the in-and-out of my breathing and the rumpety-tump-pump of my heart. Well, alright, the rumpety of my heart, anyway.

She walked back to my desk and took a gun out of one of the drawers, a little Kenju Steelie that Ma had put into my pocket one night after she'd held up a liquor store. She pointed at me.

Good. Now I finally felt really comfortable. "Why are you doing this?" she wanted to know. "I'm not doing anything, sister. Tell you what, though. You can toss me the heater and I'll point it at you, if you want me to be doing something."

"Don't wise me! How could you work for a snake like LaSiv?"

"I don't." I said. What the hell? It was true. She looked honestly surprised at that.

"Then . . . . I don't-" she stammered. "Never actually met the bastard. I owe his uncle a favor, though."

"What did he ask you to do? Just so we get this clear."

"You jumped ship on some flick before he could finish the damn thing. He wants to finish it. 'Find her,' he says. I'm good at finding people. That's about the size of it."

"That's it? That's all you had to go on?"

"That's what I get paid for, sweetie. I'm good. The best."

"It was a snuff film." Ow. I should've seen that coming. Of course, I didn't. Well, that changes things. A lot of things, actually. Okay, everything. She could tell, too, because she put the gun back down on the desk.

"You get it, now?"

I nodded. I had thought this whole shebang was almost over. That's what I get for thinking. Now I had to refigure things. "One question, first," I thought out loud as usual. "Why are you here, now? Why didn't you just drop me off and bolt for points unknown with the cash?"

"You're the dick. You tell me." That was a plenty good enough answer in my book. Okay, I had done all the refiguring I needed. It was time to get busy.

I got on the blower and buzzed the switchboard operator. "Sadie, get me Festus LaSiv, Tarsus Building. There's a doll." I waited as she did her job. A big, stupid voice came on the line and pissed me off right away.

"LaSiv? . . . Well, get him, flunko, I ain't got all goddamn day!" I waited some more. A nasally-nosed voice whined into the phone and made me feel like showering.

"LaSiv? Wichita. Yeah, yeah, I got her, yeah. I'm comin' over. Yeah, yeah, roll 'em, action, yeah, yeah, yeah."

I hung up. I picked up the Release Treats from the desk. Obviously Bella had found them. I checked my pockets for tough guy treats. Damn, I was hungry. Forget it, wimp. There'd be plenty of time for the nose-bag once this was all over.

"You stay here. Shoot anybody who tries to get into my goddamn office. Up to and including yours truly. I'll make sure to pick up some Bul-O-Stop before I come back."

I grabbed the cash and cuffed it to my wrist. She grabbed my head and kissed me, hard. I wished I was an actor so I could pretend I was into it, but I wasn't. My heart was still griplocked by a chocolate shoot-em-up angel in a red dress.

Bella slapped me. It felt good. Damn good.

"That's for luck. Now get the hell outta your office."

She slammed my door in my face, and I was a runaway train bound for Trouble Station.

I stopped only briefly on my way to the Tarsus Building to pick up a can of Bul-O-Stop from Fuckamo's Corner Store. There was a goddamn special going on, so I got a free can of Frik-Shun with it. Lucky me. I had never used it before, and I couldn't think of a damn thing it might be useful for, but I stuck it in my pocket anyway 'cause you just never fuckin' know.

The Tarsus building was tall. Not the tallest in Tough City, but that was on purpose. Same problems as trying to be the toughest in this city. If you're the tallest, you always have other buildings stepping to you, pulling bricks, and cutting you down in the middle of the night. The Tarsus was pretty damn tall, though.

And green. Green was no color for a goddamn skyscraper. I got queasy as I walked into the lobby, and so I had to throw up on the doorman.

Riding up in the elevator, I tried to think of a plan, but I've never had one before, so I lost that idea, but quick, before I got confused. I just make shit up. It's what I do, and people love me for it. Well, I love me for it. Besides, I had a suitcase full of cash cuffed to my wrist, and that made me feel like a hotshot.

I strutted my stuff around the tiny elevator. Attitude was everything. I was on top of this goddamn situation.

The elevator doors opened on the gabillionth floor onto a cavernous studio. There was expensive pretentious-looking shit all over the place.

"So this is how movies are made," I thought.

I sighed deeply as my dreams of being a big star shattered like a falling snow globe.

Not really. Just kidding.

Festus LaSiv was standing there. He was just about as I pictured him, which was damn spooky. He must have thought that oiling your entire body down was somehow a good thing. He looked like a goddamn sewer rat, and he knew it. Stewie and Reekie were there, too, flanking Festus, as were a couple of Goons-4-Hire that I supposed were there for show. There was a dame hanging off Stewie's arm, so I knew at once that she wasn't for real.

"Hey, boys," I directed at Idiot & Co. "What d'ja do wrong to get stuck with Festus duty?"

"Can it, shitheel!" countered Stewie.

His gal went to fix herself some scotch.

"Where's the slut, Wichita?" asked Festus, nervously, lips smacking.

Stewie's gal came back with the scotch and scowled.

I decided to ignore Festus for as long as I could just to piss him off.

"Who's the twist, Stewie-chan?"

He grinned broadly like he had been waiting for me to ask, which of course, he had.

His gal lit a cigarette and let it dangle from the corner of her mouth until it was almost perpendicular to the floor.

"Oh, she's way outta your class, Wichita."

His gal put one hand on her hip and twirled a string of pearls with the other. Basic Virtua-Moll, no vox-option. I knew Stewie could barely afford Basic, let alone vox-op.

"Wichita!" burst Festus, the grease literally spraying from his lips. "The bitch-whore actress! You said you'd bring her skinny ass here, to me."

I was enjoying this. And I had a feeling it was only going to get better.

Stewie's gal slapped his face and glared.

"I'm sorry, what is your goddamn part in all this?" I asked the giant rat.

The Goons-4-Hire snickered. They were already paid up though the day.

Stewie's gal hung off his arm.

"I'm the director of this film. I'M FESTUS LASIV! The Beak's nephew, hnnnnn?"

Why is it that Pixiville-types always gotta call a movie a film?

"Oh, why didn't you say that in the first place? I wouldn't a been wasting all a your goddamn time if I'd a known. Here's what I brought you."

I held up the case, the word "Ransom" facing me.

"It's a grip bag full of money. You'll never believe this, but I put that actress under my pillow last night and when I woke up this morning I found this case instead."

I remembered at this point that I hadn't actually checked the contents of the case, but dammit, I trusted that taxi driver, and, hell, I don't trust anybody. Not you, not him, and definitely not that other guy. But Merry Hashida was an Eighth Generation Bloodfeuder, for crying out loud like a girl. He wouldn't light a fuse under me.

Stewie and Reekie stared at me like I was crazy, and they weren't entirely wrong. Festus narrowed his beady little eyes, and the Goons-4-Hire stared off into space.

Stewie's gal, having reached the end of her loop, went to fix herself a scotch again.

Festus smiled, which was just plain disgusting.

"Well, Mr. Wichita, I don't know how long it took you to come up with this plan, but I see several faults: One, I'm betting that corn-fed cock-hole is waiting back at your place, which I'm sure Reekie and Stewie will be most happy to visit; two, we'll take that money, anyway, thank you very much; and three, well, I don't suppose you've a planned contingency for your early demise, now have you?"

What the fuck was he talking about? I didn't have a plan. I was just going to bust his goddamn melon.

Something was bugging me.

"You guys know of anything really jumpy?" I asked

"Prepare to die, Wichita! And here, in glorious Megatechnicolor! Roll Camera! Action! Guards! Seize him!" Boy, he just didn't even try. Reekie, Stewie, and the Goons just looked at Festus like he was crazy. Stewie's gal came back with the scotch and scowled. "Get him! Kill the detective, now! Do it NOW!" I made the first move. "Hey, Stewie, watch this magic trick." I stared his gal down and snapped my fingers, while my other hand went for a release treat. She sultried over to me and tried to sit on my lap, even though I was standing up.

Stewie's jaw dropped and he reached at his belt, fumbling madly with a little box clipped there. "Forget about it, Stewie. Your Virtua-Moll works fine, good as the real thing; that's your problem. Even Basics can tell the difference between a loser and a winner. And boy, can they smell money."

And with that, I slipped the Symbi-O-Cuffs a treat and heaved the suitcase over their heads and out the window.

The Moll went after it like a goddamn barracuda. Stewie tried to stop her, and it was the last idiot play he would ever make. It was almost touching: Stewie standing between his gal and the window, a moment before she took them both outside. Poor Stewie. I hoped he at least got a little virtual nookie on the way down. But I had stayed at this party too damn long. I made for the door and was out in the hall before you could say "terminal velocity."

No time to wait for the elevator, I broke for the stairs. I braked at the top and looked down. They spiraled down all the way to the bottom like a crazy straw. I started down and coated myself with Bul-O-Stop, the stairs offering bupkis in the way of cover. Damn their inanimate no-cover-offering hides. About two floors down, I felt the first bullet hit me. I shook it off and looked up. It was a miracle they hit me at all. The two Goons-4-Hire were at the top of the stairs, halfheartedly pointing their rental rods down at me, only aiming about half the time. They got paid per swing, not for RBIs, so they were just squeezing 'em off as fast as they could, pretty much at random, especially since no one was watching. I could always respect a good goldbricker.

I was about to continue my descent when a building fell on me. I looked up through the onslaught of fists raining down and saw a big mass of Goon in the requisite black suit. He was exercising all sorts of fancy–if ineffective–moves on my goddamn person. LaSiv must have alerted the security on each floor to stomp one DeCameron Wichita, last seen footing it down the stairs as if his life depended on it. The Goon took hold of my shoulders and marched me with a Stomping Simon. I flattened. He plopped me with a Frog Flip. I gasped. He zapped me with an Alien Stun Punch. I frizzled. He tried to chump me with a Change Maker. I shot him with my gun.

He died.

I was taking the stairs five and six at a time until I heard a bullet whine off the wall next to me. I'd whine, too, if I was a bullet, waiting around in a draughty gun all day for someone to light my fire and sink me into something warm, only to have him just louse it up in the end by bouncing me off of a goddamn cold stone wall. I looked over the handrail and saw Reekie about seven floors down, waving a big heater and racing up the stairs like some freakish . . . racing-up-the-stairs guy. He must've taken the elevator down. I stopped at the next landing and improvised.

I flipped a table out from under a chintzy vase of plastic flowers. I yanked the can of Frik-Shun out of my pocket, shook it briefly and coated the tabletop with a silvery mucous-like substance. I flipped the table over and shoved it sled-style off the landing and down the stairs. I threw myself on top of it as it went over the edge, and that's when the Frik-Shun kicked in like liquid lightning. Suddenly, I was a goddamn speed machine, rocketing down the stairs in a childhood fantasy come truer than true.

Goons-4-Hire were decorating the stairs below, eager to show how useful they could be if they cared a hoot. I was eager to shoot them, but it was all I could do to keep the table pointed in the right direction. Goons went tilt-a-whirl as I bashed into them, gaining speed with every step.

Reekie looked up and I saw him see me bearing down on him like an avalanche. I saw him see that he had nowhere to run. I saw him set his legs wide, stand his ground, and take a bead on me like a goddamn professional. I felt every round he fired hit me, and thanks to the Bul-O-Stop, I could be objective and admire his skill, of which he actually had big, fat, bagsful. I was moved to applaud, but I was afraid to let go of the fucking table legs.

All I could do was pull up on the front of the table. I felt the bump, but I never looked back. Well, that's what you get, I suppose. One second you're a faithful sharkboy, trying to earn a living, and the next, you're poorly-laid stair carpeting.

I was going so fast that I was riding less on the stairs and more up on the wall every time I went into a turn. And I was picking up even more speed, having too much goddamn fun to worry about what happened when I got to the bottom, so I just closed my eyes and screamed like a girl 'til I realized I had bottomed out and was shooting toward the lobby like gangbusters. I could see Goons piled up in front of the main door with the express purpose of getting in my way. Big Fun. Monkey Fun. The table was lickety-splitting straight at the Goons. I let go of the legs, stood up, and spread my arms wide as my grin. And at the ends of my arms were arms: Miss Dreadbolt and Miss Densha. Gentlegoons, meet the ladies. The D Sisters barked introductions like rottweilers on speed, and the security guards that had gathered there in the lobby were thrown aside like so many husks of dried security guard.

I erupted from the building, smoke trailing from my guns, and Goons trailing from my table. To the right, I caught sight of Stewie's Virtua-Moll. The control box on Stewie's hip had been badly damaged in the fall, as had Stewie. The Moll still had some life left in her, though. She was trying desperately to make off with the grip bag–my grip bag–but the wrecked control box kept telling her to slap a scotch, scowl off Stewie's arm, and to light her string of pearls and dangle them from the corner of her mouth.

Sliding out into the street, I kissed my ladies, put them to bed, then pushed the activation button on the Cuff on my wrist. Its partner, attached to the grip bag, flew out of the Virtua-Moll's claws and into my waiting arms. She screamed in silent torture and glared her shoe at me.

I stepped off the table just as it slowed to a stop in the middle of the street. I heard the screech of screeching tires, and looked up to see a familiar face looking at me through the windshield of the car that had almost ruined my lucky streak. I kicked the table towards the curb.

"Thanks, Rosebud," I said.

Pausing only to shake about ten pounds of lead from my suit, I leapt into the back seat of the car. Tires started a-screeching once more and we were gonesville.

"Haa, Ha, Haaaaaaaah, Ha, Haaah, my friend, I almost kill you! Ha, Haaaah!"

And I remembered at that moment that today was my birthday.

Well, happy birthday to me, I thought. Best party I've ever had. Merry Hashida was laughing heartily. I sat back and had a good goddamn laugh myself.

TEN

I kicked in the door, and she shot me in the face; but that's what I had told her to do, so I had been expecting it. Or rather, if I had remembered that I had told her to do just that before I busted in, I would have been expecting it. So, let's just say I was sort of expecting it and call it even. I had things to do, damn you. I flicked the bullet out from under my eye, and, not for the first time that day, thanked the kind people at Bul-O-Stop.

"DeCameron! Sorry."

She was a good shot and looked great with a gun, so I forgave her, but I couldn't help thinking that somewhere, out there, my Angel was probably filling some poor sap full of lead, and why couldn't that lucky Joe be me?

"What happened? You've still got the money!"

I'm not sure about this, but if reverie means daydreamin', then she shook me from my reverie.

"I'm gettin' you out of here. Let's go-go."

"Alright," she said, all trusty in the eyes, and I wondered what I could possibly have done to make her that way.

My coat was all swissed from bookoo bullets so I ditched it and grabbed my second favorite jacket from a hook on the wall. She grabbed her jillet and said, "I'm ready."

She was great to go and knew how to travel weightless. I liked that. She grabbed my hand, excited, like a kid going to the zoo, or some goddamn place that kids go to.

At that moment, a door opened behind her and a man with a gun walked in. I yanked her behind me as he raised the gun and fired, so fast that I barely had time to regret changing my jacket. Return gunfire erupted from between my legs, and I tried to remember when the hell I had learned how to do that; but it was just Bella, flat on the floor, gun out in front of her, lighting the gunsel up from guggle to zatch. He fell. We left even before I realized that he had come in through a door that had never been there before.

Merry Hashida was still waiting when we got downstairs. We would've been shit-out-of-luck if he hadn't. We jumped in the back and hauled ass out of there.

I had told Merry where we would be going and asked him to make a call for me besides. Now all we had to do was sit and wait. I didn't know how to sit and wait, so I was lucky that the taxi door opened and another guy with a gun tried to join us. I kicked him right in his ding-a-rooni, and he left as easily as he had come in—only I hope more painfully, at the speed we were going.

"Who are these guys?" Bella asked.

"I dunno. Must be a leak somewhere," was my witty response.

We sat back-to-back, facing our respective doors like sentinels, for a long time. Merry wasn't making it any easier, either, swerving back and forth across the road, until we noticed that Merry had only one hand on the wheel, and the other was vying for a gun with a man who must have come in his side door.

Bella had my gun up, lickety-split and blazing, but her burst aid was being hindered by the sheet of glassteel between the front and back seat. I pushed her back against the seat and kicksploded the window by her head. Then I went out after.

Squatting on the ledge with Bella hanging on to my belt from the inside, I grabbed at the side door handle and yanked it open. Reaching in, I flailed until I snatched a handful of coat–which I hoped didn't belong to Merry–and jerked, hard. The mystery gunman came out like a goddamn weed. I swung him away from the taxi and into the grille of a monstrous oncoming Bobo Truck passing us in the opposite direction. I felt it ruffle my coat as it went past, which is too close even for my abbreviated definition of comfort.

I slid back through the window and into the back seat. I hardly had to sit and wait at all before the taxi came to a halt in front of a building so tall you couldn't see the top from the bottom, nor the bottom from the top.

I hustled Bella outside and went over to Merry's window, hoping that this fracas might have, in part, influenced his career move to Tough City in a negative way.

"Haaa, Ha, Haaaaaaaah! See how I am big Tough City taxi driver, now, DeCameron Wichita! Hah, Haaaaaah! No big deal for me! Haaaaaaaah!"

I wished I could use my birthday wish to wish that he had been here to see Tough City on a tough day. Today had been a mother-lovin' cakewalk. He'd never make it out on his own. Not him. Not here. No way. He'd be better off if I broke his neck right here, and pushed his car into a goddamn abandoned quarry.

"Haaaah! For you, DeCameron Wichita. Haaaaaah!"

He flipped me a Chinese coin and split my lip for me, all from the driver's seat of his taxi. I fell on my ass. Maybe he would make it here, after all.

"Ha, Ha! Hah, h-haaaaah! DeCameron Wichita! Next time I have new Tough City wife! Yes! Ha, ha! Haaaaa!"

"Yeah, you knock 'em dead, there, Merry. There's a Tough City broad out there for you, somewhere."

Then we had a Moment. And if you ever tell anyone about this, I'll find you and make you sorry. We both smiled.

"Ha!" we yelled.

I grabbed Bella and we ducked into the building. This one was plain and grey, and my gut congratulated me for my upgrade in taste.

Waiting for the elevator, I said to Bella, "He's a tough guy."

Bella smiled, mostly to herself, which was a cryin' shame because I woulda liked a little more of it than I got. The elevator dinky-danged and we got in. The elevator rushed towards the sky like an eager soul to Heaven, except I'm betting that this elevator did it a sight more often than souls from Tough City.

"This'll probably take a little while," I said. "This is the-"

"Armitrage Building. The tallest building in Tough City. For now. I know. Just because this is the first time you've brought me here, doesn't mean I've never been here before. I was a tourist, once. What are we doing here, now?"

"You just have to trust me."

"Okay."

Cripes, that was easy.

"It's for your own good," I added.

"Now, that phrase, on the other hand, always worries me," she told me, looking at the floor.

The elevator slowed and dinky-danged to a stop a few floors from the roof. The doors slid open, and a man with a gun walked through them.

"Oh, for the man-boy luvva Bert! What in Gog and Magog is going on!?" I grumbled. Then I just hauled off and grip-kissed him good and hard in the chops with the ransom money and grabbed Bella's hand.

"Come on, sweetie, we're takin' the stairs."

We ran around the corner to a door marked "Da Stairs." It opened, and a man with a gun walked though. There was definitely a leak somewhere. Without breaking stride, I shoved him down da stairs as described on da door. I heard his neck break his fall as we climbed. Almost to the landing, I saw a door there begin to open, and took the last few steps in one leap, landing on the landing like you're goddamned supposed to, and slamming the door quite rudely on a hand holding a gun.

Only a couple more floors to the top. The door on the next landing began to open before we had even begun on the stairs, and so we ducked back around the corner. Shots rang out from above, and bullets whistled by us, ricocheting around the stairwell like angry steel hornets.

Bella fired a few shots in response, but neither of us had a clear shot. Unless she hit him by accident, we might be here for a while, and we just couldn't afford to hang around.

"Oh, fuck this situation, Bella. This is about to become a commercial for Bul-O-Stop. Get behind me."

She did, and I charged up the rest of those stairs like a bullet myself, throwing those goddamn clowns down the stairs as I went. Somebody in house cleaning was going to be pissed tomorrow morning. And, finally, we broke through to the roof. It was quiet. I knew it wouldn't last. I walked Bella to the middle of the roof and handed her one of the Symbi-O-Cuffs, along with the grip bag.

"Put it on," I said.

"Why?"

"Just trust me one more time."

"Okay. Where's the other one?" she asked. Smart kid.

"I gave it to Merry."

"Why's he got it?"

"He had to give it to Junior."

She looked at me funny. "Ju-?" she almost asked. And then she shot straight up into the night sky, and that was that.

The door to the roof opened with a bang. Well, almost that. Festus and some Assorted Goons–harder ones, I suspected, than he had had at today's embarrassing encounter–swarmed through the door and started to cover the rooftop. The Assorted Goons carried Assorted Guns, all of which looked big enough to unstop the Bul-O-Stop I was wearing. Come on, Junior.

"Wichita! Where's the girl? You promised me the god-damn stinking whore! You promised!"

Come on, Junior.

"I did?" Damn I was smooth.

"You're dead!! Roll cameras!"

Shit. Come on, Junior! It's my goddamn birthday! I looked up. Nothing. I heard the clack-chacking and buzz-whirring of guns and cameras preparing for action.

Then all I heard was a roar, and we all watched as a building rose up next to the one we were all standing on, which, I'll remind you, was, at least for the moment, the tallest goddamn building in Tough City. Then, a voice from heaven or a voice from hell:

"FESTUS!"

Festus looked up like he had been caught doing something naughty. Which I have to say honestly that I thought he had been.

"FESTUS! THIS IS YOUR UNCLE JAMES!"

It wasn't a building. It was The Beak's Edison Landmass. Hallelujah for non methynoil-efficient mega-barge technology.

"IS THIS PART OF YOUR DOCUMENTARY FILM PROJECT, FESTUS?

Festus wasn't saying anything. Unless you consider shitting yourself conversation. "FESTUS, YOU'RE THROUGH." I saw Festus swoon and crumble. "DECAMERON!" I looked up and gave a little wave.

"SOMEONE CALLED AND TOLD ME IT WAS YOUR BIRTHDAY, TODAY!" Ropes had been dropped from various ports in the Edison, and impeccably trained men in black (of course) were rappelling down to the roof. The Assorted Goons got the hell out of their way as they reassembled into a crisp formation and stood facing me, like a brace of knives.

I looked up again and nodded, sheepishly, as if he could see me. "HER NAME IS MOXIE. MOXIE L'AMOUR." I opened my mouth and snapped it shut almost immediately. My angel had a name. Moxie. "HAPPY BIRTHDAY, DE-CAMERON WICHITA!" The dangerous blacksuits began to sing, then. Happy goddamn birthday to me.

TOUGH CITY

ELEVEN

Under the sun's bastard glare, I trudged down the snarling sidewalk towards a twisted intersection in a hard-bitten area of this hard-biting city. It seemed a long-ass time since I had been down to Stickie's old place to get anything to read. Actually, it had been only a couple of days. The last few days were the kind of days that change all the days that come after. And in those last few days, I'd been thinking. Really thinking. Of Moxie.

I'm good at finding people, but I was afraid to look for her. I wanted to believe in her, but I kept telling myself she wasn't real. The ache in my heart told me different, and I wished I could tell it to shut the fuck up. And the crazy fact is that I've seen her a lot since. In stained glass windows, on medallions around people's necks, gracing the fronts of T-shirts everywhere. MOXIE RULES.

Moxie LaMoor. A myth, a legend, a savior, and nothing at all. Not for me, anyway, bucko.

I got to the kiosk and checked out my new paperbastard. He could've been Stickie's identical twin, or at least some sort of inbred relative. He eyed me suspiciously. I asked him for a goddamn racing form out of nostalgia and spite, and he gave it to me. I spotted a thin newzine that read, "VEN-

DETTA: The BloodFeuder's Weekly," and asked him for a goddamn copy of that, too.

"You ain't no Bloodfeuder," the paperbastard said, but he handed me what I asked for. Lucky him.

"No," I agreed. "Just keeping tabs on a friend."

I paid the bastard and had turned to leave, but stopped, then turned back. I still had something on my mind.

"Hey, paperbastard, maybe you can help me out. What's really jumpy? For example, if somebody said to you, 'He was jumpy as a ... ' What do you think? Jumpy as a frog? Jumpy as a Streb Fiend? What?"

"Eat shit, ass boy." he replied.

I tossed him a Chinese coin and split his lip for him, and left feeling that much more at home.

On the way to the Grindstone, I passed a flyer that caught my eye. I pulled the bastard paper away from my face and went to tear the goddamn thing to shreds, but stopped. I stopped because it was a flyer for a jazz performance. I didn't much like jazz, or it had at least always made me feel stupid, but this one intrigued me.

Headlining at the Medjugorje Rodeo Club tonight was a musician named Jumpy Yasa.

I showed up late at the club that night. I talked to the bruiser at the door. Apparently Jumpy Yasa was in the middle of his set. So much the better, I thought, not particularly enjoying what I heard. I sat at a table by myself and watched him, not knowing what I was looking for, but knowing that I wouldn't be able to take much more of this goddamn noise. I wanted a drink.

And then, a voice at my ear. "May I recommend a shot of Tick Tock Blue? It might help you enjoy tonight's performance a little more. It'll help you get in synch with the musician, and by that token, the music."

Bella.

"Yes."

Dammit, was I thinking out loud again? I turned to face her. She looked good. Even better than when she had left me alone, atop the tallest building in Tough City, to fight the bad guys.

"So, how's Junior?" I asked, to have something to ask.

"He's sorry."

"Good."

"Thank you, DeCameron."

I shook my head.

"I'm here with the rest of the crew. The ones that got away." She gestured to a corner where a pretentiously ragtag group raised their glasses in my direction.

"It looks like this film's going to get made. What with the storyboards Andy sketched before he died, and Yasa's score. Andy knew Yasa had to do the score. And, of course, with . . . your money . . ."

"Just send me a ticket when I can come and see it."

"Of course, of course," she agreed.

"Gonna have any porn in it?"

"No, DeCameron," she frowned slightly.

"Good."

She smiled.

"I think I'll have one of those drinks, now." I told her.

"Good, I'll have one sent over. I promise the music'll sound great when it kicks in." There was a pause, and then, "You'll find her, DeCameron, I know it."

"Yeah, I'm good at finding people."

But Bella was gone, and in her place, the drink. I turned to raise a toast to the crew, but they were gone, too, no doubt retired to some V.I.P. room in the back, waiting for Yasa to finish. I sipped at my Tick Tock Blue for the remainder of the gig.

And damned if she wasn't right.

EPILOGUE

The vintage black Derengetyev slid through the Tough City night like a shark in a cloud of squid ink. During the day, it might have attracted attention, but now it went unnoticed. Lucky for the unnoticers. The lights from the iconoplex danced across its skin as it passed, momentarily giving it a halo that seemed somehow out of place and yet...natural. The car stopped, and a figure emerged, her skirts flowing around her like blood in the water. And she went in.

Must even angels pray, sometimes?

Inside the iconoplex, she walked by station after station, pausing only briefly before one that bore her very own face. If she smiled, it went hidden behind the gauzy red veil that swirled in front of her mouth. Imagine then, beneath it, brilliant white teeth glaring from dark skin. Go on, imagine.

She moved on, until she had reached the far end of the 'plex. There she dropped to one knee and pressed the button by her foot.

Music began to play, soft music, the kind of music foreign to the world outside these walls. She was bathed in a red glow and was suddenly surrounded by floating figures. Fat little babies with wings.

And here, for a moment, Moxie LaMoor prayed for Love.

Or maybe she was just resting. Killing'll take it out of a person. Even the toughest. But maybe.

Then, she was gone. The Derengetyev roared to life outside as the fat little babies disappeared, and the lights faded, and the music died, and the iconoplex was dark once more.

THE END

www.ingramcontent.com/pod-product-compliance
Lightning Source LLC
Chambersburg PA
CBHW060126260626
47160CB00005B/2037